The No

A powerful d
and scan

THE DYNASTY

Eight siblings, blessed with wealth, but denied the
one thing they wanted—a father's love. A family
destroyed by one man's thirst for power.

THE SECRETS

Haunted by their past and driven to succeed,
the Wolfes scattered to the far corners of the globe.
But secrets never sleep and scandal
is starting to stir....

THE POWER

Now the Wolfe brothers are back, stronger than ever,
but hiding hearts as hard as granite.
It's said that even the blackest of souls can be
healed by the purest of love....
But can the dynasty rise again?

**Each month, Harlequin Presents® is delighted to
bring you an exciting new installment from
The Notorious Wolfes. You won't want to miss out!**

A NIGHT OF SCANDAL—*Sarah Morgan*
THE DISGRACED PLAYBOY—*Caitlin Crews*
THE STOLEN BRIDE—*Abby Green*
THE FEARLESS MAVERICK—*Robyn Grady*
THE MAN WITH THE MONEY—*Lynn Raye Harris*
THE TROPHY WIFE—*Janette Kenny*
THE GIRL THAT LOVE FORGOT—*Jennie Lucas*
THE LONE WOLFE—*Kate Hewitt*

Eight volumes to collect and treasure!

With his good arm, Alex reached and drew her near.

He saw her eyes flare and knew a moment when she might have told him to back off and let her be. But then the breath seemed to leave her body, her lids grew heavy and he saw her heart glistening there in her eyes. He was right. This situation—this maddening push and pull—couldn't go on. Now was the time to end it. And end it his way.

Even as Alex's head slanted over hers and Libby drifted off into the caress, some weak, desperate part of her cried out that this should not, *could not,* happen. But as the kiss deepened she forgot the reasons why. The slow velvet slide of his tongue over hers, the way his hands pressed her gloriously near...

This may be dangerous, but it felt so infinitely right.

Her palms ironed up over his bare, hot chest at the same time his hands pressed down over her back. His head angled as he curled over her, his touch sculpting her behind, hooking around her thigh and urging it to curl around his hip as his pelvis locked with hers. She felt the glide of his hand scooping around her thigh, sliding lower toward her knee—

Breathless—terrified—she yanked away.

Oh, God, she'd vowed this wouldn't happen again.

She didn't want him to know.

Robyn Grady

THE FEARLESS MAVERICK

 **Harlequin**®

TORONTO NEW YORK LONDON
AMSTERDAM PARIS SYDNEY HAMBURG
STOCKHOLM ATHENS TOKYO MILAN MADRID
PRAGUE WARSAW BUDAPEST AUCKLAND

Recycling programs
for this product may
not exist in your area.

ISBN-13: 978-0-373-23782-1

THE FEARLESS MAVERICK

First North American Publication 2011

Copyright © 2011 by Harlequin Books S.A.
Special thanks and acknowledgment are given to Robyn Grady for her contribution to The Notorious Wolfes series

All about the author...
Robyn Grady

One Christmas long ago, **ROBYN GRADY** received a book from her big sister and immediately fell in love with the story of Cinderella. Sprinklings of magic, deepest wishes come true—she was hooked! Picture books with glass slippers later gave way to romance novels and, more recently, the real-life dream of writing for Harlequin Books.

After a fifteen-year career in television, Robyn met her own modern-day hero. They live on Australia's Sunshine Coast, with their three little princesses, two poodles and a cat called Tinkie. She loves new shoes, worn jeans, lunches at Moffat Beach and hanging out with her friends at www.Harlequin.com. Learn about her latest releases at www.robyngrady.com and don't forget to say hi. She'd love to hear from you!

Books by Robyn Grady

Harlequin Presents®
2881—DEVIL IN A DARK BLUE SUIT
2850—NAUGHTY NIGHTS IN THE MILLIONAIRE'S
      MANSION

CHAPTER ONE

THE moment Alex Wolfe's car went airborne, he knew the situation was bad. That's 'serious injury' or possibly even 'get ready to meet your maker' bad.

He'd been approaching the chicane at the end of a straight at Melbourne's premier motor racing circuit and, misjudging his breaking point, he'd gone into the first turn too deep. He'd tried to drive through the corner but when the wheels had aquaplaned on standing water, he'd slid out and slammed into a tyre stack wall, which provided protection not only for runaway cars and their drivers but also for crowds congregated behind the guard rail.

Like a stone spat from a slingshot, he'd ricocheted off the rubber and back into the path of the oncoming field. He didn't see what happened next but, from the almighty *whack* that had spun him out of control, Alex surmised another car had T-boned his.

Now, as he sliced through space a metre above the ground, time seemed to slow to a cool molasses crawl as snapshots from the past flickered and flashed through his mind. Anticipating the colossal *slam* of impact, Alex cursed himself for being a fool. World Number One three seasons running—some said the best there'd ever been—and he'd broken racing's cardinal rule. He'd let his concentration slip. Allowed personal angst to impair his judgement and screw with his performance. The news he'd received an hour before climbing into the cockpit had hit him that hard.

After nearly twenty years, Jacob was back?

Now Alex understood why his twin sister had persisted in trying to contact him these past weeks. He'd been thrown when he'd received her first email and had held off returning Annabelle's messages for precisely this reason. He couldn't afford to get wound up and distracted by—

Driving down a breath, Alex thrust those thoughts aside.

He simply couldn't get distracted, is all.

With blood thumping like a swelling ocean in his ears, Alex gritted his teeth and strangled the wheel as the 420-kilo missile pierced that tyre wall. An instant later, he thudded to a jarring halt and darkness, black as the apocalypse, enveloped him. Momentum demanded he catapult forward but body and helmet harnesses kept him strapped—or was that *trapped?*—inside. Wrenched forward, Alex felt his right shoulder click and bleed with pain that he knew would only get worse. He also knew he should get out fast. Their fuel tanks rarely ruptured and fire retardant suits were a wonderful thing; however, nothing stopped a man from roasting alive should his car happen to go up in flames.

Entombed beneath the weight of the tyres, Alex fought the overwhelming urge to try to punch through rubber and drag himself free, but disorientated men were known to stagger into the path of oncoming cars. Even if he *could* claw his way out, procedure stated rescue teams assist or, at the least, supervise occupants from any wreck.

Holding his injured arm, Alex cursed like he'd never cursed before. Then he squinted through the darkness and, in a fit of frustration, roared out in self-disgust.

'Can we try that again? I know I can cock up more if I really set my mind to it!'

Claustrophobic seconds crept by. Gritting his teeth, Alex concentrated on the growl of V8s whizzing past, rather than the growing throb in his shoulder. Then a different group of engines sped up—medical response units. Surrounded by the smell of fumes and rubber and his own sweat, Alex exhaled a shuddery breath. Motor racing was a dangerous sport. One of the *most* dangerous. But the monumental risks associated with harrowing speeds were also the ultimate thrill and the only life to which Alex had ever wanted to ascribe. Racing not only gave him immense pleasure, it also provided the supreme means of escape. God knows there'd been plenty to run from growing up at Wolfe Manor.

The muffled cries of track marshals filtered through and Alex came back to the present as a crane went to work. Bound stacks of tyres were removed and soon shafts of light broke through.

A marshal, in his bright orange suit, poked his head in. 'You all right?'

'I'll live.'

The marshal had already removed the steering wheel and was assessing what he could of the car's warped safety cell. 'We'll have you out in a minute.'

To face a barrage of questions? The humiliation? And at some stage he'd have to tackle that other problem, which had set off this whole shambles.

'No chance of leaving me here, I suppose.'

The marshal took in Alex's sardonic smile and sent a consoling look. 'There'll be more races, son.'

Alex set his jaw. *Damn right there will be.*

The Jaws of Life arrived. Soon, sure hands were assisting him out and a world of fire-tipped arrows shot through that injured joint. Biting down, Alex edged out of the debris aware of fans' applause resonating around the park. He let go supporting his right arm long enough to salute to the cheering crowd before sliding into a response unit.

Minutes later, inside the medical tent and out of his helmet and suit, Alex rested back on a gurney. Morrissey, the team doctor, checked out his shoulder, applied a cold press, then searched for signs of concussion and other injuries. Morrissey was serving up something for the pain and inflammation when team owner, Jerry Squires, strode in.

The son of a British shipping tycoon, Jerry had lost an eye as a child and was well known for the black patch he wore. He was better known, however, for his staggering wealth and no-nonsense attitude. Today, with his usually neat steel-grey hair mussed, Jerry spoke in gravelled tones to the doctor.

'What's the worst?'

'He'll need a complete physical evaluation… X-rays and MRI,' Morrissey replied, his glasses slipping to the tip of his nose as he scribbled notes on a clipboard. 'He's sustained a subluxation to his right shoulder.'

Jerry sucked air in between his teeth. 'Second race of the season. At least we still have Anthony.'

At the mention of his team's second driver, Alex pushed to sit up. Everyone was jumping the gun! He wasn't out of the game yet.

But then the pain in that joint flared and burned like Hades. Breaking into a fresh sweat, he rested back on the elevated pillows and managed to put on his no-problem smile, the one that worked a charm on beautiful women and bristling billionaires.

'Hey, settle down, Jer. You heard the man. It's not serious. Nothing's broken.'

The doctor lowered his clipboard enough for Alex to catch the disapproving angle of his brows. 'That's still to be determined.'

A pulse beat in Jerry's clean-shaven jaw. 'I appreciate your glass-half-full attitude, champ, but this is no time for a stiff upper lip.' Jerry glanced out the window and scowled at the churning weather. 'We should've gone with wets.'

Alex flinched, and not from physical pain. In hindsight, granted, he should have opted for wet-weather tyres. He'd explained his rationale to the team earlier when other pit crews were changing over. Now he'd reiterate for the man who forked over multiple millions to have him race as lead driver.

'The rain had stopped ten minutes before the race began,' Alex said, feeling Morrissey's eagle eye pressing him to button up and rest. 'The track was drying off. If I could make it through the first few laps—get a dry line happening—I'd be eating up the k's while everyone else would be stuck in the pits changing back to slicks.'

Jerry grunted again, unconvinced. 'You needed extra traction going into that chicane. Simple fact is, you called it wrong.'

Alex ground his back teeth against a natural urge to argue. He hadn't called it wrong…but he had made a fatal error. His mind hadn't been one hundred percent on the job. If it *had* been, he'd have aced that chicane *and* the race. Hell, anyone could drive in the dry; handling wet conditions was where a driver's ability, experience and instinct shone through. And usually where Alex Wolfe excelled. He'd worked bloody hard to get where he was today—at the top—which was a far cry from the position he'd once filled: a delinquent who'd longed to flee that grotesquely elaborate, freakishly unhappy English manor that still sat on the outskirts of Oxfordshire.

But he'd left those memories behind.

Or he had until receiving those emails.

While Jerry, Morrissey and a handful of others conversed out of earshot, Alex mulled over his sister's message. Annabelle had said Wolfe Manor had been declared a dangerous structure by the council and Jacob had returned to reinstate the house and grounds to their former infamous glory. Images of those centuries-old corridors and chunky dusty furniture came to mind, and Alex swore he could smell the dank and sour bouquet of his father's favourite drop. The veil between then and now thinned more and he heard his father's drunken ravings. Felt the slap of that belt on his skin.

Clamping his eyes shut, Alex shook off the revulsion. As the eldest, Jacob had inherited that mausoleum but, if it'd been left to him, Alex would gladly have bulldozed the lot.

Still, there'd been some good times as kids growing up. Alex had surrendered to a smile when Annabelle's email also mentioned that Nathaniel, the youngest of the Wolfe clan—or of the legitimate children, at least—was tying the knot. A talent behind the lens for many years now, Annabelle was to be the official photographer. Alex had followed recent news of his actor brother in the papers…the night Nathaniel had walked out on his stage debut in the West End had caused a terrific stir. Then had come his Best Actor win last month in LA.

Alex absently rubbed his shoulder.

Little brother was all grown up, successful and apparently in love. Made him realise how much time had passed. How scattered they all were. He best remembered Nathaniel when he was little more than a skinny kid finding his own form of escape through entertaining his siblings, even at the expense of a backhand or two from the old man.

Voices filtered in and Alex's thoughts jumped back. Across the room it seemed Jerry and

Morrissey had finished their powwow and were
ready to join him again.

His eyebrows knitted, the doctor removed his
glasses. 'I'll attempt to reduce that joint now. The
sooner it's intact again, the better. We're organising
transport to Windsor Private for those follow-up
tests.'

'And when the tests come back?' Alex asked.

'There'll be discussions with specialists to as-
certain whether surgery's needed—'

Alex's pulse rate spiked. '*Whoa*. Slow down.
Surgery?'

'—*or* more likely some rest combined with a
rehabilitation plan. It's not the first time this has
happened. That shoulder's going to need some
time,' Morrissey said, tapping his glasses at the
air to help make his point. 'Don't fool yourself it
won't.'

'So long as I'm back in the cockpit in time to
qualify in Malaysia.'

'Next weekend?' Morrissey headed for his desk.
'Sorry, but you can forget about that.'

Ignoring the twist of fresh pain, Alex propped
up on his left elbow and forced a wry laugh. 'I
think I'm the best judge of whether I'm fit to drive
or not.'

'Like you judged which tyres to kick off the
race?'

Alex slid a look over to Jerry Squires at the same

time his neck went hot and a retort burned to break free. But no good would come from indulging his temper when the frustration roiling inside of him should be directed at no one other than himself. No matter which way you sliced it, he'd messed up. Now, like it or not, he needed to knuckle down and play ball…but only for a finite period and largely on his own terms. Because make no mistake—if he had to miss the next race, he'd be in Shanghai for Round Four if it killed him.

First up he'd need to shake any press off his tail. After such a spectacular crash, questions regarding injuries and how they might impact on his career would be rife. The photographer jackals would be on the prowl, desperate to snap the shot of the season—the Fangio of his time, the great Alex Wolfe, grimacing in pain, his arm useless in a sling. Damned if he'd let the paparazzi depict him as a pitiful invalid.

Privacy was therefore a priority. Any recuperating would happen at his reclusive Rose Bay residence in Sydney. He'd source a professional who understood and valued the unique code elite athletes lived by. Someone who was exceptional at their work but who might also appreciate a lopsided grin or possibly an invitation to dinner when he was next in town, in exchange for which she would provide the medical all clear needed to get him back behind the wheel in time for Round Four qualifying.

As the painkiller kicked in and the screaming in his shoulder became more a raw groan, Alex closed his eyes and eased back against the gurney.

When his shoulder was popped back in and those initial tests were out of the way, he'd set his assistant, Eli Steele, on the case. He needed to find the right physiotherapist for the job. And he needed to find her fast. He'd lost far too much in his life.

God help him, he wasn't losing this.

CHAPTER TWO

As HER car cruised up a tree-lined drive belonging to one of the most impressive houses she'd ever seen, Libby Henderson blew the long bangs off her brow and again spooled through every one of her *'I can do this'* and *'There's nothing to be nervous about'* affirmations.

As her stomach churned, Libby recalled how not so long ago she'd been a supremely self-confident type. Nothing had frightened her. Nothing had held her back. That verve had propelled her to dizzy heights—a place where she'd felt secure and alive and even admired. Twice Female World Surfing Champion. There were times she still couldn't believe that fabulous ride had ended the way it had.

From an early age she'd taken to the surf. Libby's parents had always referred to her as their little mermaid. Growing up she'd trained every minute she could grab—kayaking, swimming, body surfing, as well as honing her skills on a board.

Nothing had felt better than the endorphins and burn she'd got from pushing beyond her limits.

Being a world champion had been the ultimate buzz—fabulous sponsors, high-end magazine spreads, the chance to speak with and even coach youngsters eager to surf their way up through the ranks. Out ahead, for as far as she could see, the horizon shone with amazing possibilities. Her accident had changed that.

But, thankfully, there'd been a life after celebrity and elite athlete status, just a different life. When she'd overcome the worst of her accident, she'd thrown herself into the study she'd previously set aside and had attained a Bachelor of Health Sciences in Physiotherapy at Sydney's Bond University. She was beyond grateful her determination and hard work was paying off—today better than she'd ever dreamed.

As she swerved around the top end of the drive now, Libby recalled this morning's unexpected phone call. None other than Alex Wolfe, the British-born motor racing champ who'd come to grief at the weekend, had requested her services. Mr Wolfe's assistant, an efficient-sounding man by the name of Eli Steele, had relayed that he and Mr Wolfe had researched specialists in her profession extensively and had decided that her credentials best suited Mr Wolfe's current needs with regard to the shoulder injury he'd sustained.

Libby had to wonder precisely what credentials Eli referred to.

She worked almost exclusively with injured athletes but she'd never treated anyone near as renowned as this man. Perhaps Alex Wolfe, or his assistant, was aware of her former life, Libby surmised, slotting the auto shift into park and shutting down the engine. But had they dug deep enough to unearth how the final chapter of that part of her life had ended?

After opening the car door, Libby swung her legs out. Pushing to her feet, she surveyed the magnificent ultra-modern home as well as the surrounding pristine lawns and gardens. Rendered white with ultramarine and hardwood trims, the Rose Bay double-storey mansion spanned almost the entire width of the vast block. She imagined numerous bedrooms, each with their own en suite and spa bath. An indoor heated pool would provide luxurious laps during winter while an Olympic-size outdoor pool with trickling water features and, perhaps, a man-made beach would be the go during Sydney's often scorching summer months.

Straightening the jacket of her cream and black-trim pants-suit, Libby craned her neck. A grand forecourt, decorated with trellised yellow-bell jasmine and topiaries set in waist-high terracotta pots, soared around her. Her eyes drifting shut, she inhaled nature's sweet perfume and hummed out a sigh. In her sporting heyday, she'd earned good money but nothing compared with this unabashed show of wealth. Of course, the lucrative runoffs from the Alex Wolfe range of aftershave, clothing and computer games would contribute handsomely to his fortune. Charm, money, movie-star looks. Hell, Alex Wolfe had it all.

A thoroughly sexy voice, with a very posh English accent, broke into her thoughts.

'I agree. It's a cracking day. Perhaps we ought to chat out here.'

It started in her belly...a pleasant tingling heat that flooded her body in the same instant her eyes snapped wide open. On that extensive front patio, directly in front of her, stood a man. *The* man.

Alex Wolfe.

An embarrassing eternity passed before her stunned brain swam to the surface. Frankly, she'd never experienced a sight—a *vision*—quite like the one openly assessing her now. His lopsided grin was lazy, carving attractive grooves either side of a spellbinding mouth. His hair was a stylishly messy dark blond, the length of which curled off the collar of a teal-coloured polo shirt. And what about those shoulders! Mouthwateringly broad. Ubermasculine.

And let's not forget, Libby warned herself, sucking down a breath, the *only* reason she was here.

Stopping long enough to think about which foot

to put forward first, Libby pinned on a warm but businesslike smile and moved to join her newest client, whom, she noticed now, also wore a navy blue immobiliser sling.

'I believe you were expecting me. I'm Libby Henderson. I was just admiring your home and gardens.'

He surveyed the vast front lawns and nodded as a gentle harbour breeze lifted dark blond hair off his brow. 'I always enjoy my stints in Australia,' he said. 'The weather's brilliant.' Gorgeous soft grey eyes hooked back onto hers as he cocked his head. 'I'd offer you my hand but...'

'Your right shoulder's giving you problems.'

'Nothing too serious,' he said, stepping aside to welcome her in.

Entering the foyer, which gave the modest size of her Manly apartment a decent run for its money, Libby considered his last comment. If Mr Wolfe's injury had been enough to land him in hospital and warrant subsequent intensive treatment ordered by his team doctor, clearly it was serious enough. Her job was to make certain that full range of motion and strength returned and, despite any downplaying on his part, that's precisely what she intended to do. Men like Alex Wolfe wanted to get back to it, and *now*. She understood that. Unfortunately, however, sometimes that wasn't possible.

Forcing herself not to gape at the storybook

multi-tiered staircase or the mirror-polished marble floors, Libby instead turned to her host as he closed the twelve-foot-high door. She suppressed a wry grin. Must be the butler's day off.

'Can I offer you a refreshment, Ms Henderson?'

As he passed to lead her through the spacious white, almost austere vestibule, Libby's thoughts stuck on what should have been a simple question. But his tone implied that rather than coffee, any refreshment he offered might include something as social as champagne.

'I'm fine, thank you,' she replied, unable to keep her gaze from straying to the fluid style of his gait in those delectable custom-made black trousers as he moved off. Would he detect any peculiarities in her stride if their positions were reversed—she in front, he behind? But surely a man who'd dated supermodels and at least one European princess wouldn't be interested enough to notice.

'We'll talk in the sunroom.' Stopping before a set of double doors, he fanned open one side and she moved through.

After he'd closed this door too, he headed for a U-shaped group of three snowy-white leather couches. Beyond soaring arched windows sat that magnificent outdoor pool she'd imagined as well as a glamorous spa and stylish white wicker setting. A pool house, which mimicked the main building's design, looked large enough to accommodate a family of four as well as friends. Positioned beyond the pool area was a massive storage block—she suspected a huge garage. All the world knew Mr Wolfe liked his cars.

He gestured to the closest couch. 'Please make yourself comfortable.'

Libby lowered back against the cushions and set her feet neatly together. Rather than taking up position on the opposite couch, Alex Wolfe settled down alongside of her. A flush crept up her neck and lit her cheeks. This man's magnetism was a tangible, remarkable thing. His proximity to her on this couch couldn't be deemed as inappropriate— at least an arm's length separated them—and yet she couldn't ignore the *pull*. Not that Mr Wolfe would purposely be sending out those kinds of vibes. He was simply…well, he was only…

Oh, dammit, he was *sexy*—beyond anything she'd ever experienced before.

As a film of perspiration cooled her nape, Libby edged an inch away while, holding the sling's elbow, Alex stretched his legs out and crossed his ankles. His feet were large, the shoes Italian. She noticed those things nowadays.

'So, Ms Henderson, what do you have for me?'

'I've studied the MRI scans,' she began, her gaze tracing the line of that sling, 'as well as the orthopaedic surgeon's report outlining the details of the injury. Seems your shoulder didn't suffer a complete dislocation, but rather a subluxation. Do you know what that means?'

'My shoulder didn't pop completely.'

She nodded. 'In layman's terms, that's precisely it.'

When that amazing subtle smile lighting his eyes touched his mouth, Libby's tummy fluttered and she cleared her throat. *Yes, he's an incredibly attractive man but, for God's sake, concentrate!* Her goal here wasn't to get all starry-eyed but to have Alex Wolfe walk away from this episode fully recovered and bursting with glowing reports of her services. Hopefully, then, more of his ilk would follow and her reputation in her present career would be secured.

When she'd returned to her studies, she'd decided she wanted to work with elite athletes, that special breed that needed someone who not only understood how their bodies worked but also their minds, and who were prepared to do whatever it took to get back on top. Libby only wished she'd been given that option.

Centring her attention again, she threaded her fingers and set them on her lap. 'Your medical records outline ligament damage to that shoulder in your teens.'

His eyes clouded over for an instant, so stormy

and distant she might have mentioned the devil. But then his smile returned, and more hypnotic than before.

'I came off a motorbike.'

She nodded. A natural thrillseeker, of course he'd have started out on two wheels. 'I see.'

'Do you like motor sports?'

'I was more a water girl.'

'Swimming? Skiing?'

That flush returned, a hot rash creeping over the entire length of her body. Feeling colour soak into her cheeks, she glanced down, unclasped her hands and smoothed the centre creases of her trousers. They weren't here to discuss her history.

'I have another appointment this afternoon, so perhaps we'd best stay on point.'

His gaze sharpened, assessing her, and he sat back. 'I imagine your practice keeps you busy, Ms Henderson.'

'Busy enough.'

'But not on weekends.'

'I work some Saturdays.'

'Not Sundays?'

She blinked. 'You think you'll need me Sundays too?'

'Let's make it every weekday for now.'

'Much of the work you can do without my help. Every second day would be sufficient.'

'Every week day,' he reiterated before smiling

again. 'Don't worry, Ms Henderson. I promise my current predicament is extremely short-term.'

Libby's breath left her lungs in a quiet rush. This man was a living legend. Revered by millions all over the world. He was the sporting hero that boys chasing one another in parks pretended to be. Was he being intentionally snide? Or just plain 'I am invincible' arrogant? Libby knew better than most.

No one was invincible.

'We were discussing your previous injury,' she went on in an implacable tone, 'which could well have made you more susceptible to subsequent injuries. Let me explain.' She shifted back against the cushions. 'A joint dislocation, or *luxation* from the Latin, occurs when bones that join become displaced or misaligned usually through a sudden impact. The joint capsule, cartilage and ligaments become damaged. A subluxation, as occurred in your situation, Mr Wolfe, is a partial dislocation, which can occur as a result of previous damage to the surrounding structures of the shoulder. Either way there will be a weakening of the muscles and ligaments which need physiotherapy to help stabilise the joint.'

He was looking at her, his head slightly angled, a peculiar, flattering gleam in his eyes.

'I see.'

She held her breath against an unbidden flare

of emotion, cleared her throat and focused again. 'With your hands on the wheel, the impact from the accident jarred your right humerus, which then sat anteriorly from the—'

His deep soft laugh interrupted her. 'Rewind a little, doc.'

'I'm not a doctor.' She wanted to be clear on her qualifications. 'I have a Bachelor of Health Sciences with honours and am a member of the Australian Physiotherapy Association.'

'And for now you are the lady who holds my future in the palm of her hand. I'll call you "doc." With your permission, of course.'

Libby stiffened. Talk about pressure. But then, he was paying the bill. She gave a hesitant half-shrug.

'I suppose…if it makes you feel more comfortable.'

His gaze dipped to her lips, then caught her eyes again. 'So—*doc*—you were saying.'

'Your humerus—' She stopped and bunched one hand to demonstrate. 'The *ball* slid partially out of its joint and needed to be manipulated back into the centre of your glenoid cavity, or socket.' She cupped her palm, pushed her fist in and locked the 'ball,' then disengaged it again.

'Right. The ball—' his own hand bunched '—goes into the socket.' He fit his big hard hot fist inside her still-elevated palm.

At the instant of contact, Libby's internal alarm blared and she jerked away.

Their eyes locked—his questioning, hers, she knew, wide and exposed. That tingling in her belly had intensified and the suddenly sensitive tips of her breasts tightened and ached.

But when one corner of his mouth hooked up the barest amount, Libby was brought back. As casually as possible, she scooped some hair behind an ear and willed her cantering heartbeat to slow. Crazy to even consider but…

Was he *flirting* with her? She couldn't be sure. He was a superstar and…

It'd been such a long time.

Her last intimate relationship had ended four months after her accident. She'd thought fellow pro surfer Scott Wilkinson had been the sexist man alive, but Scott was an amateur compared to Alex Wolfe. This man's power to captivate with a simple look, the slightest touch, was palpable. She'd like to meet the woman who was immune to the magic of that smile. Charm was as instinctive to this man as his taking a corner at death-defying speeds. That wasn't to imply he would in any way be interested in checking her track out, so to speak.

More to the point, *she* wasn't interested in a quick spin with him either.

Schooling her features, Libby straightened her spine and focused on business. 'We'll need to concentrate on a series of strengthening rehabilitative exercises.'

'Sounds good.'

'When would you like to begin, Mr Wolfe?'

'Call me Alex.'

A perfectly reasonable request, she decided, noticing how his grey eyes seemed to sparkle at her nod of accent. 'What if I set up a timetable—?'

'I thought we could start tomorrow.'

'Tomorrow's fine.' Her voice lowered to a serious note. 'I'm sure I don't have to tell you that we'll need to work hard. Consistently.'

'I've no doubt you'll bring me through in time.'

Frowning, she cast her mind back. Had she overlooked something?

'In time for what?'

'I'll miss Round Three this weekend.' A muscle in his cheek flexed twice. 'Can't be helped, I'm afraid. Round Four's three weeks subsequent to that.'

Libby almost laughed. He was joking. But while his expression might be relaxed, the set of his square jaw was firm. He'd never been more serious in his life.

'I was told you'd been declared unfit by your team's doctor to drive professionally for at least six weeks.'

'We'll prove him wrong.'

She sat forward. He should be set straight.

'Your trackside physician wasn't able to perform the reduction. As you'd have been told many times now, delay can cause complications. An axial view showed stripping of the inferior glenoid and rotator cuff tearing…'

Her words dropped away as any patience she'd seen in his eyes on the subject cooled.

'My assistant informs me,' he said, 'that your clients think you perform miracles.'

'I'm not a saint, Mr Wolfe.'

'*Alex*. And, believe me, I'm not after a saint.'

His eyes smouldered and that hot pulse in her belly squeezed and sizzled. When the beating slid to a lower dangerous point, Libby pushed to her feet, too quickly as it turned out. She tipped to one side and threw out an arm to steady herself. But Alex Wolfe was already there, standing close, an arm circling her waist, his solid frame effortlessly providing the support she needed.

She was five-six, but she had to arc her neck way back to look into his face…which was a mistake. When those entrancing lidded eyes fused with hers, she imagined that his hold around her middle cinched, bringing her front to within a hair's-breadth of his…close to his chest…to those legs.

Giddy, she broke his hold and took two steps back.

As she willed the fire from her face and got herself together, he asked, 'Are you all right?'

'Perfectly. Thank you.' Shifting the bangs off her cheeks, she gathered herself and resumed a businesslike air. 'I presume you know where my practice is.'

'All treatments will be conducted here.'

Her brows shot up. 'My equipment's at work.'

'I'll be honest.' His free hand slid into his trouser pocket and his legs braced wider apart. 'I'm concerned about the press. I have enough on my mind without watching out for headlines speculating on whether I'm a washed-up cripple.'

Her insides wrenching, Libby flinched.

In the second it took to compose her expression, Alex frowned as if he'd glimpsed and wondered at her lapse. With knees locked, she offered an indulgent smile.

'I understand you might want to shield yourself. But I'm afraid—'

'Everything you need will be brought in. I'll have my assistant organise it. And I'll double your fee to cover any inconvenience and time difficulties.'

She shut her dropped jaw.

Was she reading him right? *Double your fee...? We'll prove him wrong...? You'll bring me through...?* Did he think he could bribe her into cutting short his treatment so he could make his Round Four? Clearly Alex Wolfe wasn't familiar with the terms *caution* or *compromise*. He knew only one way to get things done. *His* way. If she didn't agree to his conditions—his offer—no doubt he'd find someone who would.

Which left her two choices.

She could bow to the inevitable, agree that all work be carried out on his private premises and take the fortune he offered as well as give the all clear when he deemed, whether he was fit to return to driving in her opinion or not. Or she could tell him she couldn't be manipulated by his charm or his pride. That her ethics were more important to her than money. More important than anything.

But there was a third option.

Decided, she looked him in the eye. 'I'll speak with your assistant. Get the ball rolling. We'll start tomorrow morning.'

A shadow swept over his expression, so fast she almost missed it. She recognised the emotion. Disappointment. He'd thought she'd put up more of a fight before capitulating to his terms, even for show's sake. Pity she couldn't set him straight, but that would come…when the time was right.

She headed for the door. 'I'll be back in the office in half an hour. Your assistant can call me any time after that.'

With long fluid strides he caught up, a satisfied smile tilting his lips. 'I do believe I'll enjoy working with you, doc.'

Doc. Walking side by side down the hall, Libby grinned.

'Perhaps I ought to wear a white coat and stethoscope when I call next,' she said, a slightly mocking edge to her voice.

'Feel free to wear whatever makes you comfortable. I will.'

'Oh, there won't be much need for clothes,' she said, stopping before the front doors. 'On your part, at least.'

His hold on the handle froze.

Swallowing the grin, she brushed his hand aside, opened the door and stepped out. 'See you tomorrow. Nine sharp.'

Walking away, she felt his surprise and curiosity drilling her back. But if her last comment was loosely inappropriate, she was okay with it. He'd needed to be pulled up and using his own level of language.

Alex Wolfe didn't know how well she understood his mind. She knew about burning passions. About setting a goal and never losing sight of it. She also knew how it felt to lose the capacity to chase and hold onto your dream. To have to reinvent yourself and leave that other more natural you behind.

Six weeks rehabilitation? Hell, Alex Wolfe didn't know how lucky he was.

But slow and steady won the race. *This* race

anyway. She'd get him into a routine, he'd feel the positive results and when the time came she'd make him see how detrimental—possibly catastrophic—returning to the track too soon could be. Until then she'd be on her guard. She couldn't deny that those subtle looks, his unmistakable body language, his casual touch, affected her, and Alex knew it. He assumed he could manipulate her, charm her, perhaps even intimidate her into getting what he wanted.

Unfortunately for Alex Wolfe…not a chance.

Libby slid into the driver's seat. She was about to turn the ignition when her stomach twisted, like it had earlier when he'd tossed off that unconscious slap in the face. Her hand ran down her left thigh, over the patella. Then her fingertips traced the line where she and the lower limb prosthesis became one.

Washed-up cripple…

Long ago she had finished crying and asking herself, *What did I do to deserve this?* With the support of family, friends and professionals she'd moved from beneath those dark clouds of self-pity. Helping to rehabilitate others had brought new and worthwhile meaning to her life. But sitting here, remembering the gleam in Alex Wolfe's eyes when he'd looked at her that certain way, she couldn't mistake the pang in her chest or the choking thickness in her throat.

Her hand skimmed the shin she couldn't feel. Would Alex Wolfe see her as less of a woman if he knew?

CHAPTER THREE

LEANING his good shoulder against a patio column, Alex kept his eye on Libby Henderson's silver sedan as it looped the circular drive and headed out. An intrigued smile lifted one corner of his mouth.

Ms Henderson was an attractive prospect, particularly with those large amber-coloured eyes that seemed to both cloak her emotions as well as swirl with boundless possibilities. Her hair, which flowed past her shoulders in soft waves, was a captivating silvery blond, a consequence, no doubt, of a lifetime spent in Australia's surf-and-sun conditions. Of medium height, her lithe figure had curves in all the right places. If she'd tried to hide that fact beneath her designer business suit, she'd failed and she knew it.

Perhaps best of all, he thought as he watched her car disappear beyond the auto iron entry gates, Libby Henderson had spunk.

She'd as good as accepted his offer—to work

here on him, *with* him. However, she'd let him know that he didn't intimidate her, even if they were aware of each other in a primal man-wants-woman way. When her palm had cupped his fist, she'd felt the zap as much as he had. But her comeback regarding the insignificance of what clothes he did or did not wear during their sessions had been priceless. Few people could pull him up like that. Coming from Ms Henderson, he couldn't say he minded.

Clearly, she was the right person for the job. With his past, he didn't wait around for miracles, nevertheless he had faith that Libby Henderson's clients believed she could work them. Regardless, he would have little trouble persuading her and, as a consequence, others that he was indeed fit to drive again when he deemed it should be so. And if she needed a hand in helping her decision along, he wasn't opposed to the idea. In fact, now that he'd met her, he was more than intrigued by the prospect.

Recalling the natural wiggle in her walk, he pushed off the column.

Until that time, he needed to focus elsewhere. Needed to keep busy. Tomorrow midday, a video-conference with the Australian CEO of his best-selling signature-brand aftershave was scheduled. Before then, he'd go through projection figures for an additional anticipated range. Along with earnings from his extensive investment portfolio, he certainly didn't need the money, but a man would be a fool not to strike when his iron was hot. Current and potential sponsors agreed: Alex Wolfe was *steaming*. He intended to keep it that way.

About to head in, he pulled up. Eli Steele's sleek black sports car was slinking up the drive. Grinning, Alex crossed back to the patio's edge. Not only was his assistant smart in a business sense, he had a good head for cars. Eli wouldn't be working for him if he didn't.

'I take it that was your physiotherapist driving off,' Eli said, easing out the driver's side door. 'How'd it go?'

'Well.' After Eli made his way up the steps, Alex clapped his friend on the back with his free hand. 'You did a fine job finding her.'

Eli drove a set of fingers over his scalp, ruffling his neat dark hair. 'So she's on board?'

'I've explained I need to be back in the seat no later than Round Four.' Two weeks shy of the six weeks the team doctor had insisted upon, which would leave him in a good position to retain his title.

Inside the vestibule, they hung a right and sauntered down the hall which led to Alex's home office.

'And she said she can accommodate?' Eli asked.

'Was there any doubt?'

'Only on my part, it seems.'

Frowning, Alex stopped. 'Run that by me again?'

Eli kept walking. 'Don't get me wrong. I'm convinced she does great work, but from what I've read she seems to have a granite mindset as well. I didn't think she'd roll over and agree to your time frame that easily.'

Outside the billiards room, Eli waited for his boss to catch up.

Digesting the information, Alex began to walk again. 'You sound unhappy about her being onside.'

'You want to race,' Eli explained, 'and you want to win. Clearly you can handle pain. But, Alex, you don't want to risk this injury getting worse. This is the second time that joint has given you trouble. Third time it'll be easier to damage still. If that happens you could be out for a lot longer than six weeks.'

They entered the office, its walls lined with framed shots capturing some heady moments on the track as well as the winner's podium—holding up a plate at Monaco, shooting champagne over an ecstatic crowd. Alex's favourite trophy by far was a homemade medal, which hung on a haberdashery store's dark blue ribbon. Made out of an inexpensive key ring and a portion of a wheel spike, the good-luck charm had been given to him many years ago by his mentor, a man to whom Alex owed everything—Carter White. Encouragement, belief. Carter had given the rebel teen Alex had once been the tools needed to succeed, which included the gift of a caring father figure Alex had sorely lacked at home. He really ought to pick up the phone and call Carter sometime.

Crossing to his desk, Alex collected the documents he'd received from that CEO and the bold *Alex Wolfe* logo caught his eye. Everyone was eager to see how far his brand-name net would fly and Eli was great to bounce new ideas and strategies off. He was more than an assistant; Eli was a first-class friend. They'd known each other only three years and yet Eli was closer to him than any of his brothers. Not that Alex blamed anyone for that…or, rather, he blamed no one other than the man who had single-handedly torn his own family apart: William Wolfe, may he rot in hell.

And he was seriously giving too much thought to all this lately but, for once, he couldn't seem to avoid it.

Staring blindly at those documents, Alex recalled how he'd waited until he'd left the hospital to reread Annabelle's email and compose an adequate reply.

Great to hear about Jacob's return and Nathaniel's upcoming nuptials, it had said. *Can't believe he's old enough to tie the knot! Will be in contact again soon. Hope you're well. Love to you, Alex.*

He'd thought about phoning; he had her number. But he knew Annabelle favoured email. Frankly, in this circumstance, so did he. Not that he and Annabelle didn't speak every couple of years or so...but never about that night. Not about what a different girl Annabelle was now from the lively chit she'd once been.

Alex lowered into his high-back leather chair, only half hearing Eli's last remark.

'...I'm sure Libby Henderson explained that to you.'

Alex's thoughts slid all the way back. Eli was talking about the increased chance of incurring a similar injury to his shoulder in the future.

'I'll keep up the exercises,' Alex said, 'and whatever else she prescribes.'

'As long as you don't screw it up permanently in the meantime by going back to the track too soon.'

Alex tossed a wry look around the walls, covered with victory memorabilia. 'I think I've done fairly well so far.'

But when Eli's dark blue gaze dropped and he rubbed the scar above his temple the way he did whenever he had something more to say, Alex blew out a breath and set the document down on the desk with a slap.

'Spit it out.'

Eli edged a hip over the corner of the polished rosewood desk and gave a shrug that said he was perplexed. 'I guess I'd expected Libby Henderson to put up at least a half-decent fight.'

In truth, Alex had expected that too. She'd almost agreed *too* easily to his generous offer. Nevertheless, 'Money's a strong motivator. With that kind of dosh on the table and the endorsements I'll flick her way, she'd be a fool not to jump at this chance.'

'I wouldn't have thought she'd be motivated by money any more than you are.'

'Why's that?'

'You seriously don't recognise the name?'

Alex rolled it over in his mind and came up a blank. 'Sorry.'

'Elizabeth Henderson was World Surfing Champion a few years back.'

Alex recalled her radiant can-do glow, the determined look in those swirling amber eyes, not to mention the alluring beach-babe hair and tan. Elizabeth Henderson, world champion surfer? He grinned. Sure. It fit.

'I had no idea,' he admitted. 'Water sports aren't my thing.' He and Libby had even had that discussion. 'I don't much follow female sport either. Do they televise women's surf championships?'

With a sardonic grin, Eli collected the document Alex had set aside. 'For a smart man, you're one hell of a chauvinist.'

Alex held his heart. 'You've wounded me.' Then he offered up a conciliatory smile. 'Don't worry. I'm on top of it. When Libby Henderson sets her mind to something, she does it her way and leaves the rest for dead. Which can only bode well for her performance as a physio.'

Dark brows knitted, Eli was flicking through the document, sifting through data. Eli was a hound for tracking down and assimilating facts. Which begged the question...

Eyes narrowed, Alex swung his chair one way, then the next. Finally he asked, 'Why didn't you tell me about Libby Henderson's past first-up?'

Eli continued analysing the pages. 'I wanted you to meet her without any preconceptions.'

'I don't see how knowing about her sporting acumen could hurt.'

When Eli kept his focus on the document, Alex's antennae began to prickle. Had being cooped up without driving privileges brought out a paranoid streak? Or was there something more to Libby Henderson? Something that Eli, for some curious reason, preferred his boss not discover?

He'd set out to hire someone who would be

malleable to his needs. That objective hadn't changed. And yet after a single meeting he couldn't deny he was intrigued to learn more about this former surf queen turned sports star physio. Was his curiosity in part due to the fact that Libby reminded him of his sister? She and Annabelle conveyed a similar almost regal reserve, although Alex well remembered his sister in her younger years—open and vibrant. So eager to experience all life had to offer. He'd wager Libby harboured a more effervescent side as well. Either way...

Eli leaned over to point out some anomaly in the document but Alex found his thoughts still on Libby.

An attractive option. Boundless possibilities.

Yes. When Ms Henderson visited next, he'd be certain to dig deeper.

CHAPTER FOUR

HALF an hour later, Libby walked through the entrance of her city office. Behind the front desk, her twenty-one-year-old receptionist, Payton Nagle, flicked back her waist-length chestnut hair and beamed out an enthusiastic smile.

'So*oooo*…how was the superstar?'

Containing a grin, Libby crossed over and scooped up the morning mail from the counter's top shelf. 'Still shining bright.'

'What's he like?' Eyes round, Payton tipped forward. 'Is he as sexy in real life as he is on the TV?'

'I'd have to say sexier,' Libby replied, matter-of-factly. The man was *so* sexy, it was criminal.

Falling back in her seat, Payton sighed long and hard at the ceiling. 'That strong square jaw, that deep to-die-for Brit accent…Honestly, Libby, I don't know how you stopped from swooning.'

'I'm a professional, Payton,' Libby said, shuffling through letters and invoices. 'Professionals aren't allowed to swoon.' Or rather they weren't allowed to let those kinds of unprofessional feelings show.

She set down the mail and drilled her receptionist with her most serious gaze. 'Remember, not one word about my appointments with Alex Wolfe to anyone. He wants the press to think he's flown back to the UK or the paparazzi would be all over this. He doesn't want the situation with his shoulder made out to be any worse than it is.'

Didn't want to be projected as a cripple.

Shaking off that thought, Libby stretched toward the keyboard to check her email account while Payton crossed her heart to seal the promise. 'Did you tell him about your surfing?'

Libby recalled her thoughts from earlier, when she'd left Alex Wolfe and his premises. Other than the everyday reminder below her left knee, 'That part of my life's behind me.'

Payton's brows tugged together. 'But being a world champion…it's something you'd have in common.'

'I'm not there for chitchat.'

Or here, for that matter.

Setting her mind squarely back on business, Libby moved toward her office. A long low whistle, the sound of a missile falling, came from behind.

Hands on hips, Libby rotated back.

Payton was twirling a thick strand of hair around an index finger. 'You really like him, don't you?'

Libby's eyes bugged out. *Like* him?

'Payton, he's impossibly arrogant. Consumed by his own celebrity. And besides that…' Libby's fists loosened, her inflexible look melted and, beaten, she exhaled. 'Besides that, any woman with her full quota of hormones couldn't *help* but like him.' She shrugged. 'He's *drugging*. Same way honey is to a bee.'

'I wonder…' An eyebrow arched as Payton twirled more hair. 'Are you the honey or the bee?'

Libby coughed out a laugh. If Payton was suggesting that Alex Wolfe found *her* irresistible…!

'I'm neither,' Libby replied in an end-of-conversation tone. 'I'm a physiotherapist who has a full day ahead of her. As does her receptionist.'

Moving into her office, Libby shut the door and took two calming breaths to rein in the cantering pace of her heartbeat. She and Payton might be friends but foremost she was the younger woman's employer. Someone Payton should be able to hold up as an example. Revealing a vulnerable side— the purely female side that found Alex Wolfe absurdly attractive—had been foolish. And a one-time mistake.

Crossing to her desk, Libby told herself that Mr

Wolfe had fleets of starry-eyed admirers the globe over, women who dreamed about being with him, talking to him, *doing* for him. They would also dream about how that kissable mouth might feel sensually closing over theirs, or the way he might move when he made hot, unhurried love deep into the night.

Resigned, Libby dropped into her chair.

Hell, she wasn't so different to those other mesmerised hoards. And that had to stop.

She knew Alex Wolfe's type. World Number Ones were all about staying on top. He would use anything and everything within his means to have her capitulate, wave her physio's green flag and get himself back on the track whether his injury was sufficiently healed or not. But no matter how distracting Mr Wolfe's looks and charm, she would *not* let herself be manipulated. There was only one thing for it.

Spine straight, knees together, she swept up her schedule.

From now on she would be nothing but objective in his company. Ruthlessly ethical. A consummate, non-sexual, iron-willed professional.

Ready to sort through the papers on her desk, Libby had collected a pen when a pang in her chest had her catching her breath. The thought had crept up on her like a frost on nightfall, and now that the reflection was formed she couldn't blot it out. Couldn't shake it off.

After her accident she'd thrown herself into study, then the practice. No energy was left over for window-shopping for knee-high dresses she would never wear or wondering if sometime, somewhere, she might meet someone new. She was too busy— too focused—and she preferred her life that way.

Now, for the first time in so long, she gave into the impulse, closed her eyes and remembered what it was like to be kissed by a man. How wonderful it could feel to be desired. She remembered the swell of want when tender words were whispered and steaming hungry flesh met flesh. Then she recalled the pure elation of spearing through a salt-water mountain and shooting free the other side. Her mind joined the two and drew a picture of a tall strong man, the lacy fringes of ocean waves swirling around his ankles, grey eyes smiling.

Squeezing the pen, Libby bowed her head. As well as she knew her own name, she was certain she would never return to the ocean. As much as she missed the water that was one challenge she didn't need to face. But would she ever know romantic love again?

She hadn't let herself dwell before now but, in truth, she missed the company, the sense of sharing, the special warmth of intimacy. And as silly as it sounded, she couldn't help but wonder...

What would it be like to have all that with Alex?

The next morning, her professional mask firmly in place, Libby arrived at Alex Wolfe's elite address smack on nine. As he had the day before, Alex greeted her at the door, escorted her inside, then led her into a spacious room—an elaborate home gym toward the rear of the enormous house.

Libby almost gasped. She'd seen licensed gyms less equipped than this. Every type of weight equipment, three state-of-the-art treadmills, six rowing machines, various balls, mats, presses and bars. A small double-glazed window set in an adjacent wood panelled wall indicated a sauna. Did the man host boot-camp parties? That indoor pool she'd imagined must be close by. Not that they'd be using it. She would always love the smell and look of water any way it came—sea, chlorinated or fresh from the sky. But her mermaid days were long over.

Arm in its sling, Alex sauntered over to join her. 'Should we start with a cup of strong tea before getting into the tough stuff?'

As usual that deep accented voice seeped through Libby's blood, making her syrupy warm all over. Ignoring the heat, aware of the dangers, she steeled herself, met his gaze and set her work bag on a nearby table. He might be king of his profession but during these sessions, like it or not, she was in charge.

'We'll begin with a full assessment.' She nodded at his immobilised arm. 'Now that we'll be concentrating on strengthening your shoulder, there won't be a need for that.'

With a speculative smile, Alex reached for a fastener. 'My shirt will need to come off too, I presume.'

'I'll help with the buttons.'

When she didn't hesitate to step forward and assist, his brows hiked but she didn't react. He could turn on the wicked charm all he liked, but if he'd hoped to put her off balance again today, he could think again. She'd made a pledge and she intended to keep it.

Iron-willed.

Asexual.

Professional.

With the sling removed, she deftly unbuttoned his freshly laundered chambray shirt. The subtle smell of lemons drifted into her lungs, but the scent that truly caught her senses was musky. Pure male. A scent she wasn't unfamiliar with in her everyday work. But, of course, Alex Wolfe went a mile beyond 'everyday.'

Last button attended to, she eased the shirt

off those dynamite shoulders, then manoeuvred around to release the fabric from his back. As the shirt fell away, her gaze gravitated to the muscular contours, the straight-as-a-die dent of his spine, the lean measure of his hips. Her heart began to pound. She thought she'd prepared herself but, frankly, the sight of this man half naked stole her breath away.

Thrusting back her shoulders, she once again set her mind on the specialist straight and narrow.

'Let's start with testing your range of movement.'

She asked that he first raise his arms in front, palm down, as high as possible, then at his sides. Next, internal and external rotation, with his hands behind his back.

While making notes—the ROM around the joint was not full, which meant passive work to help it improve—she said, 'Now we'll test the strength.'

His good shoulder squared. 'Ready when you are, doc.'

Navigating around to face him, Libby found herself analysing that amazing chest and powerhouse arms from a female rather than professional point of view. Big mistake. Her brain began to tingle at the same time her bones seemed to liquefy. She'd laid awake half the night telling herself she could handle whatever today might bring and yet she'd missed the turn-off coming here because she'd been contemplating precisely this moment.

Resisting the urge to wet her lips, she eased her gaze higher and met his amused look. Then one corner of his mouth slowly curved and her face flooded with heat. Caught out, she stuttered an excuse. She hadn't been ogling. Merely... *assessing*.

'You, uh, obviously work out,' she said, and then inwardly cringed.

Stupid. He was a World Number One. Of course he worked out. No doubt there'd be gyms in his other houses around the world, and the best personal trainers, as well as a food plan to sustain the mind and might of a champion.

She cleared her throat. 'What I mean to say is... despite your injury, you look great.'

His lips tilted more at the same time he seemed to move slightly closer, lean faintly nearer, and the heat in her cheeks exploded, raging out of control as that natural male scent enveloped her completely.

His gaze skimming her cheek, he murmured, 'Thank you.'

Gulping back a breath, she averted her gaze and muttered, 'You're welcome.'

She imagined that he chuckled to himself before he asked, 'Where would you like me?'

With unsteady steps, she crossed to a mirror

that covered an entire wall. 'We'll start here. You in front facing the mirror. I'll stand behind.'

He took up his position, steely legs in black athlete's shorts pinned apart. His slightly cleft chin angled up. 'How's this?'

Libby was torn between sighing and smirking at the magnificent reflection. As if he didn't know he looked better than fabulous.

'That's fine. Now hold your arms out at right angles to your body.' His arms rose easily. 'Any pain?'

'It feels…' The chiselled planes of his face pinched. 'A little weak.'

She grunted. She'd bet more than 'a little.'

'I'm going to test that strength. I'll put one hand here on the uninjured arm and the other here, on your recovering arm.'

As she laid a palm on each bicep, she felt the vibration…his chest rumbling, the sound of a big cat anticipating a full bucket of cream or, perhaps, defending it.

Locking off her imagination, she continued. 'Now I'll push lightly.'

'Would you like me to push too? You know—' his left bicep flexed twice beneath her hand '—push up?'

She met his poker-faced reflection and simmered inside. Damn the man! He'd done that little trick on purpose. This wasn't a contest or a show. Every session, every minute, counted. He needed to take this seriously.

Filling her lungs, she reassembled her patience. 'I'll push down and you try to resist.'

Gently she put weight on each arm. His left stayed parallel. His right came down.

His cool expression dissolved and a crease cut between his brows. 'That's no good.'

'With your injury, it's normal. We'll get there.'

'Yes, we will. In time for China.'

She held off gaping at his implacable tone. But she had no intention of arguing that particular point now. She had a job to do. His shoulder would be fit for a return to the track when she said it was and not a moment before.

'Would you go over there and lie down, please?'

Holding his injured arm, Alex looked her up and down, as if deciding whether it would weaken his position to comply. Then he reluctantly crossed the room, hitched up on the bed's white sheet and spread out.

Edging closer, she scanned the exquisite form lying before her and swallowed against the rapid pulse beating high in her throat. He looked even better on his back than he had standing. The rectus abdominis had been sculpted by a god. The tone of his trapesius and deltoids were exceptional. The pectoralis majors, dusted with crisp hair, were as first-rate an example as she'd ever seen—and she'd seen a few. Powerful, firm, prime flesh. Below that waist band, Libby imagined another well defined muscle and her mouth went dry.

He pushed up on his good arm and his broad shoulders slanted toward her. 'Maybe we should start with something more strenuous. You know, get the show on the road.'

'No, Alex. We shouldn't.'

His jaw shifted and eyes narrowed. 'I can't see what lying around will achieve.'

'Leave that to me.'

His gaze pierced hers, challenging, testing. Finally he rolled back down, looking like a third grader forced to face some senseless spelling bee he hadn't studied for.

He stared blindly at the ceiling. 'What now?'

Alongside of him, Libby took both his hands, which felt as hot and strong as the rest of him looked. Her fingers curled around his and she brought them to lie near his navel. She refused to acknowledge the trail of dark hair descending in a particularly tantalising line to the loose band of his shorts, much less the subtle bulge further down.

'No pain?' she asked in a remarkably composed voice.

His gaze met hers and, confident, he grinned. 'Not a hint.'

'Good. Now slowly lift your arms.'

'How high?'

'See how you go. I'll go through the exercise with you first.' With his hands sandwiched between hers, a hot pulse beating through her blood, she began to move with him. 'Up, two, three... hold and...down, two, three.' Her words were even, regulated, the opposite of her clambering heartbeat. 'How's that feel?'

'Up. Down. Up. Down.' She felt his curious gaze on hers. 'How much longer?'

'A few more times.'

Any moment she expected him to protest again but as their breathing synchronised with the movements, he seemed to accept the inevitable. So while they finished the set, she focused on his shoulder, as well as his expression for signs of discomfort. Her gaze drifted to gauge the steady breathing of that glorious chest and before she could rein her straying thoughts in, she imagined her palms gliding over that granite surface and her lips brushing those small dark discs.

Hauling herself back with a start, Libby lowered their hands a final time and took a resolute step away.

'That's it?' he asked, sounding pleased.

She patted her hair, which she'd worn in a low bun with multiple pins today. 'Now I'll show you an easy exercise to continue with.' An active as opposed to passive version of the exercise they'd done together. 'And we'll work in some remedial massages along the way.'

But he growled. 'I don't need massages. I don't want easy.'

What he really meant was, *This soft stuff is a waste of time.*

Tucking in her chin, Libby took stock.

This time with Alex Wolfe would be more difficult than she'd thought. She knew Alex was beyond eager to get back onto the track and that he was beyond confident about his abilities. She respected where that energy came from…an unconquerable winner's spirit. That quality, however, did not excuse his veiled attempt to bribe her, suggesting she convince the team doctor that he was fit and well to drive whether he was or he wasn't. Nor did it excuse that forceful tone.

Regardless, the bottom line was that she'd taken on this case, which meant she would give it her all and then some, whether Alex Wolfe appreciated her own brand of zealousness or not. If he decided their relationship wasn't working, he could sack her, but she wasn't about to quit, or double guess herself at every turn. He'd thought enough of her credentials to hire her in the first place after all.

'Alex, I appreciate your…enthusiasm, but I'm going to ask you to leave the program to me.'

'Just as long as we're in tune with what I need.'

What I expect, he should have said.

Her smile was thin. 'I know precisely what you need.'

His gaze pierced hers and she thought he might push his point to make himself clear. The simmering in his eyes said he would miss not one more race than he thought he had to. Every round he didn't drive took him further away from the means to retain his title, and anyone who tried to stop him was public enemy number one.

But then the thrust of his shadowed jaw eased, his trademark grin returned and he added in a placated tone, 'Pleased to know we're on the same page.'

They continued to work out with similar isometrics. After thirty minutes, she caught him flinching so she called an end to their first session.

'That'll do for today,' she said, heading off to collect her bag.

He was standing, hands threaded behind to allow a gentle stretch between the blades. With his brow damp from rehabilitative work his body wasn't used to, he joined her. 'So you're leaving?'

'I have other appointments.'

She was sure he wouldn't be lonely. He must have acquaintances in Sydney he could catch up with. No doubt many wore skirts.

While she found her car keys, he eased into his shirt. Leaving it unbuttoned—an unabashed encore, she supposed—he escorted her out of the gym. Halfway down the long northern hall, that enormous storage block, visible beyond a set of soaring windows, caught her eye.

Curious, she slowed up. 'What do you keep out there?'

'Three guesses.'

She only needed one. 'Cars.'

He laughed and the deep, easy sound—as warm as a blanket on a cold night—made her forget what a privileged pain in the butt he could be at times.

'Come and have a look,' he said. When she opened her mouth to object, he broke in. 'Surely you can spare five minutes.'

Libby thought it over. Her next appointment wasn't for an hour, and she was intrigued as to how many and what types of cars a motor racing champion owned. She knew Payton would be interested to hear.

Relenting, and more than a little excited, she nodded. 'Five minutes.'

His grey eyes smiled, but in a different way—as if he truly appreciated her interest—and together they walked out the house, past the magazine lift-out pool and over the immaculate emerald-green lawn.

'Where did it all start,' she asked, 'this love affair with cars and speed?'

'My father owned prestige automobiles, everything from vintage classics to top-of-the-range sports cars. Every now and then I'd take one out.'

'He must have trusted you a great deal.'

'Oh, I didn't ask. I became quite well known throughout Oxfordshire for my jaunts.'

'Known to the authorities?' He only grinned, his gaze distant and mischievous as he remembered back. 'What did your father say when he got a hold of you?'

He opened the huge end door and flicked a switch. An enormous space, filled with rows of gleaming prestige cars, materialised before them.

'What's your poison?' he asked. 'The red Ferrari F430 is extremely popular. Then there's the classic British sports car, which I can assure you is a very nice ride.'

The spectacle greeting her was so out of the world 'rich and famous,' Libby put her hand to her chest to try to catch a gasp. 'I hate to think of your insurance bill. Do you have as many cars in your other homes?'

They strolled further inside, under the overly bright lights, surrounded by automobile excellence and an atmosphere of wealth at its decadent best.

'This is my main stash. I have another healthy group hidden away in the French countryside. Some in England too.'

'Must leave your dad's collection for dead.'

Without commenting, he strolled on, and it clicked that he hadn't answered her previous question. What had his father done when he'd caught his son driving his prize cars? But then the obvious dawned and she guessed why he didn't want to speak about it.

She put a compassionate note into her voice. 'Is he still alive?'

Alex frowned over. 'Who?'

'Your father.'

He ran his left hand over the bonnet of a deep-blue muscle car. 'He's dead.'

Expecting that answer, she nodded. 'I'm sorry.'

'You must be the only person alive who is.'

Libby blinked several times and was about to ask him to explain. But his eyes were suddenly so shuttered, his face expressionless. Clearly this was a touchy subject. Seemed there was more to motoring superstar Alex Wolfe than met the eye, an obvious bitterness toward his deceased father for one. What else lay beneath his polished public persona?

But she was being no better than the press. Everyone was entitled to keep their past private, she and Alex included.

Still walking, she crossed her arms and looked down. 'I apologise. I shouldn't have dug.'

He tugged an ear and, thoughtful, focused on

some far-off point. 'Quite a bit of digging's been going on recently,' he admitted.

About his past? Who was digging? 'Someone from your family?'

'Yes. From the family.'

'Who?'

'My twin.'

'You have a twin brother?'

'Sister.'

'What's her name?'

It took a few seconds for him to answer.

'Annabelle.'

'Alex and Annabelle.' She smiled. Cute.

'She was in contact before my accident.'

'Something to do with your father?'

'His estate,' he replied. Then he turned back to face her and his demeanour purposely lightened. 'Seems our oldest brother has made an appearance out of the distant blue to renovate old Wolfe Manor before the council tears it down. A sound idea, if you ask me.'

'This is back in England? Oxfordshire?'

'An estate overlooking a quaint little village by the name of Wolfestone.'

Libby shook her head, amazed. How many people had a village named after their family? But Alex didn't seem impressed by any of it. The timbre of his voice was casual again but the light in his usually entrancing grey gaze had dulled.

'How long since you've seen this mysterious brother?' she asked, knowing she was being nosy again.

But Libby knew ghosts from the past could creep up when a person had time on their hands, and Alex wouldn't be used to being confined, cut off, the way he had been these past days. If he wanted to share—about his family and old Wolfe Manor—anything he said wouldn't go beyond her.

'Jacob left Wolfe Manor almost two decades ago. Disappeared one night without a goodbye.' He looked down at the same time his brow furrowed. But then he seemed to shore himself up, particularly when his gaze hooked onto another sporty car. 'I'd offer you a ride in my Sargaris TVR but I really need two hands to control it.'

She'd lost interest in cars. 'Do you have other siblings other than those two?'

'Three shy of a football team.'

'Do you see them often?'

'Not regularly. Never all together. I haven't seen Jacob since he left.' Alex hunkered down to inspect something that seemed to trouble him about one of the car's tyres. 'What about you?'

'Me?'

'Do you have brothers and sisters?'

'I don't have any siblings.'

'Your parents alive?'

'And well.'

'What did you do before becoming a physio?'

As he pushed to his feet, she saw a certain glint in his eye and her insides wrenched. Seemed he had a few questions of his own…questions she wasn't entirely comfortable with answering. Time to pull up the brake.

She curled some hair behind an ear. 'I didn't mean to pry so deeply. We got sidetracked and I was interested…'

Her words trailed off as he angled more toward her. The air between them seemed to crackle when he said in a deep sure tone, 'I'm interested too.'

She let out a pent-up breath. The emotion in his eyes looked sincere. But how much was she prepared to divulge? Although her accident and subsequent amputation weren't federal secrets, she'd made it her policy not to wallow in the past. She certainly didn't want pity, which was often people's first reaction.

Dismissive, she hitched up one shoulder. 'My family history isn't that exciting.'

'I'm sure being the female world surf champion would've been anything but boring.'

Her stomach pitched and a chill crept over her scalp. She felt unsteady. Worse, she felt like a downright fool. He *knew* about her past? And he'd said nothing! What other information had he gathered?

Although she was boiling inside, somehow she kept her tone civil. 'You should have mentioned that you knew.'

'Perhaps you should have mentioned it first.'

Her hands balled. He might be world famous but, honestly, who did he think he was?

'My past, Mr Wolfe, is hardly detrimental to my current career. If anything, it's advantageous.'

He quizzed her eyes and the unspoken question hung between them. *Then why not put it in your résumé?*

The uncomfortable silence stretched out. Feeling off centre—trapped—she forged a look at her watch. Way past time she was gone.

'I should leave,' she said, rearranging her bag's shoulder strap. 'I'll be late for my next appointment.'

After hesitating only a heartbeat, he nodded and agreed. 'I'll see you out.'

He moved to take her elbow. Instinctively she jerked away. Too friendly.

'No need,' she said. 'You lock up here. I'll see myself out.'

As she turned away, at the far end of the garage parked near a battered dartboard, a car caught her eye. Rusted, uncared for, the bonnet was buckled, as if the driver had slammed into a tree. What was that wreck doing among these trophies? But she wasn't about to ask. This conversation had got way too personal already.

Leaving Alex behind, she made a beeline for the garage's exit.

From now on she would keep her thoughts and questions to herself. And, as much as she could, her hands as well.

CHAPTER FIVE

Two weeks later, Alex was shunting a hand through his hair, pacing the floorboards of his home office. Libby Henderson had left thirty minutes earlier. As usual she'd been the consummate professional at their regular morning session. Had performed her duties with routine perfection.

Alex stopped and glared at his feet.

That woman was driving him mad.

Not because she was inadequate with regard to his treatments. From time to time he might hint that things weren't moving quickly enough, but in truth her slow and steady approach seemed to be paying off; his shoulder was twice as strong as it had been. His problem with Ms Henderson—what niggled him to the core—was far more complicated than that.

Other than the brief time he and Libby had spent in his garage when they'd exchanged titbits about each other's pasts, she was a clam. Tight-lipped, focused only on business and, more to the point, doing it all *her* way. Although he hadn't wanted to commit to paper his confidential proposition with regard to China—fine fodder for blackmail should it fall into the wrong hands—he believed he'd been clear when they'd struck their deal. In conjunction with therapy, he needed her help returning to the track in not six but *four* weeks. In exchange for this service, he would pay an exorbitant fee and sing her praises the world over. She'd agreed they were on the same page. However, despite her verbal acceptance of his terms, he was far from convinced that Libby Henderson was anyone's man, so to speak, but her own. That troubled him.

But there was more.

When they were together in the mornings, despite her pronounced reserve, he'd become more aware of a certain thrumming connection. The soothing sound of her voice. Her unconscious habit of curling hair behind an ear. The slant of her smile when he'd performed some exercise to her satisfaction. She'd grown on him, and the longer she maintained her emotional distance, the thicker the wall she put up, the more determined he was to knock it down. But neither charm nor mutual silence—not even obvious agitation—seemed to make a dent in her brickwork.

The homemade medal, hanging on its ribbon on the wall, seemed to call. As usual, memories of his gratitude to Carter and earliest commitment to his sport swam up. Alex couldn't change his mind about Round Four. He lived to race. To *win*. China meant valuable points that would tally toward this year's championship. So what to do about Libby? Would she or wouldn't she give him what he needed?

Other than Annabelle, he'd never met a woman like her. Polite but also unremittingly cool. This morning he'd asked how often she surfed nowadays. The look she gave could freeze the Gobi. Was conversing with him so distasteful?

Or was her reserve caused by something deeper…some past hurt perhaps? He'd never tried to penetrate Annabelle's veneer; neither brother nor sister wanted to dig around those old wounds. But Libby…

Filling his lungs, Alex hunted down his phone, punched in a speed dial and, mind set, waited to be connected. He'd been as good as locked away here, hell-bent on withholding any ammunition about his condition or imminent comeback to the press. But his arm was out of its sling. No one would guess anything was wrong with his shoulder. Frankly, he'd go stir-crazy if he didn't break out and soon.

He knew the perfect person with whom to share some R and R. The same person who needed to be asked a straight question and, in return, give a straight answer.

Phone ringing in his ear, Alex lowered into his chair, smiling.

He only needed to create the right atmosphere.

In her city practice, Libby sat at her desk, staring at a scramble of near-legible notes. Almost noon and she hadn't got close to nutting out the speech she needed to give this time next month. A formal national dinner with her peers, she wanted her words on the podium to shine and inspire. And yet here she was, scrubbing her brow, wishing she could focus on her words.

Instead she was thinking about the irascible Alex Wolfe and his penchant for being alternately charming or painfully difficult.

Each morning she'd show up at Alex's mansion, and just as routinely he would complain about whatever exercise she asked him to perform. Although his shoulder was free of its sling and they'd progressed to using resistance bands and light weights, clearly he considered the work needlessly repetitive and beneath him. But even demigods had to show humility and face their vulnerabilities sometime. Alex's time was now. Either that or he might find himself in hospital again—this time, perhaps, under the knife.

Lately, she felt at her wits' end. After that day in his garage when personal details had cropped up to momentarily misalign their relationship, she'd let him know that she was there for business and business only, and yet no matter what she suggested or how she suggested it, he seemed more committed to challenging her efforts or creating a more casual atmosphere than anything else. Clearly he didn't comprehend the possible consequences. But she wasn't about to roll over and let him run her show, even if a part of her understood his reluctance.

Doodling a shell alongside her speech salutation, Libby recalled a time when she hadn't let anyone get through to her either. Where Alex was too 'above it all,' during the first weeks of her rehabilitation she'd been filled with anger and frustration. She'd lost the surf, her fiancé…heck, she'd lost a *limb*. To her mind she didn't need to work at getting well. What was the point?

Thank heaven that phase had soon passed and she'd come out the other end valuing, beyond anything, the perseverance of people who had not only stood by her, but had also said, with both patience and courage, how things needed to be if she wanted to get the most out of life. Like those people who had helped her, she wouldn't give up on Alex, no matter what trivialising tactic he used to try to manipulate the situation. His recovery meant a lot to him. It meant a lot to her too.

A harried padding of footfalls sounded on the corridor carpet. Short on breath, face flushed, Payton rushed into the room.

'You'll never guess who's here!'

Putting a lid on her surprise, Libby calmly set down her pen and sat straighter. 'Given that blush, I'm guessing Alex Wolfe.'

A tall broad-shouldered figure was already stalking up behind Payton. Then Alex was standing in her doorway, smiling that irrepressible smile. Her autonomic reaction to his presence never failed to astound Libby. Her stomach muscles contracted, her insides warmed and glowed and, immediately light-headed, her gaze soaked up the hypnotic message in his eyes, then dipped to appreciate the intoxicating masculine tilt of his lips.

No wonder poor Payton was beside herself.

Looking as if she were about to melt, Payton kept her gaze on their visitor. 'I said you wouldn't mind if he came straight through.'

'That's fine, Payton.' Libby pushed up on slightly unsteady feet. 'The front bell just rang, if you'd like to see who it is.'

Edging around their visitor, Payton reluctantly headed off.

When they were alone, Libby skirted her desk and, leaning against the edge, crossed her arms. 'This is a surprise.'

His brows shot up. 'You don't remember?'

Libby stopped breathing. Did they have an appointment she'd forgotten? Not possible.

'Remember what?'

With that lazy delectable stride that sent her heartbeat racing all the more, he sauntered forward. 'It's our two-week anniversary.'

Libby couldn't help it. She laughed. In between being chronically difficult, Alex could also be infinitely charming.

'So it is. Happy anniversary.' Her eyebrows snapped together. 'You didn't drive here, did you?' She'd told him this morning that another couple of days off from civilian driving was safest.

'Although I'm sure I could,' he told her, 'I got a ride.'

'A taxi?'

'Limo.'

Libby's head kicked back. Hardly the transport of a man who wanted to remain inconspicuous.

'I thought you wanted to lay low?'

He shrugged. 'My accident is old news now.'

She understood his point; today's headline was tomorrow's back page small print. Although she couldn't imagine any member of the paparazzi passing on the chance to catch a celebrity of Alex's stature off the clock.

Then again Alex might have decided that now his arm was sling-free and stronger, he wouldn't mind a spot of *positive* publicity. Either way his rationale on that subject had less than nothing to do with her.

Casually inspecting her office walls—her degrees,

photos and that black-and-white aerial of Sydney circa 1960, predating the Opera House—he strolled further into the room.

'Are you busy?' he asked.

'I'm always busy.'

'But you'll need to stop to eat.'

'I usually get in a sandwich,' she said, vaguely suspicious now.

He rotated to face her. 'No sandwich today. Grab your coat.'

'I beg your pardon?'

'I'm taking you to lunch.'

Libby's hands fell to clasp the edges of the desk either side of her hips. Not for one moment had she imagined this visit was linked to anything other than his therapy. Since that day in the garage, she'd avoided any talk of a private nature. Having him acknowledge a two-week anniversary was curious enough. Now he was inviting her to lunch? She was near speechless.

She shook her head. 'I don't think it's appropriate that our relationship should include...'

But her words trailed off. Was that a puppy-dog face he was pulling?

'You don't want to hurt my feelings, do you, doc?'

'Feelings,' she announced, 'have nothing to do with it.' She rounded the desk and lowered purposefully back down into her seat. When their eyes met again, that knee-knocking smile had only spread wider.

'Would it help if I said please?'

'I'm sorry.' Collecting her pen, she pretended to focus on her notes. 'But I have work to do.'

'Client appointments?'

'Guest speech.'

'I'm good with speeches. We can discuss it over lunch.' From beneath her lashes, she saw him saunter across and her heartbeat began to flutter. 'Or I can organise take-out. We can have a picnic in here.' His attention zeroed in on a photo framed behind her. He squinted, then chuckled. 'Hey, that's *you*.'

Libby groaned. *This* is why she'd never wanted him in here. Questions. The answers of which were her business and nobody else's.

Nevertheless, she acknowledged what was obvious. 'Yes, that's me, but a long time ago.'

She braced herself, waiting for him to ask about her current surfing habits again like he had this morning; she'd rather not discuss it. Instead his gaze swept over and he smiled.

'C'mon, doc. The limo's waiting.'

She reclined back and studied him for a drawn-out moment. Finally she huffed. 'You're not giving up, are you?'

'I've done everything you've asked these past two weeks. We deserve some time-out.'

'You've done *everything* I've asked?'

At her unconvinced look, he let slip a grin. 'Well, sometimes you might've needed to ask twice...'

A runaway smile stole across her face. Then her gaze fell to her disarray of notes. She'd vowed to have this first draft down by the end of the week. But her stomach did feel empty. Maybe her brain would work better after a good meal. And that was the *only* reason she was going. Although to believe conversation wouldn't vie toward the personal was naive. She couldn't help but wonder if he'd heard from his sister about his mysterious brother again.

Giving in, she unfolded from the chair, raised her chin and stipulated, 'One hour.'

'One hour?' Alex broke into a broad smile. 'We'll discuss it over lunch.'

Twenty minutes later, Alex's chauffeur-driven limousine parked outside a quaint-looking restaurant. The high-pitched ornate roof and rattan features suggested an oriental bent. Then Libby caught a whiff of spicy aromas and saw the establishment's name.

Malaysian Pearl.

As the uniformed driver assisted her out, Libby sent Alex a look. 'Is this place supposed to be a hint of some kind?'

'I figure since I missed the race in Sepang I

ought to enjoy some of the flavours of the country
I won't get to visit this year.'

'You're a fan of Malaysian food?'

Joining her, he set his palm lightly on the small
of her back and winked. 'The hotter, the better.'

Libby moved away from his touch. She wasn't
certain he was speaking about curries.

They moved up the timber plank path, past the
peaceful trickling of a rock pebble water feature.
Inside they were seated in a private corner, which
was cloaked by palm fronds, bamboo dividers and
bordered by generous windows overlooking the
blue silk-stretched waters of the bay. The interior
reflected Eastern symmetry, simplicity and seren-
ity—a smiling Buddha sat on a podium facing the
entrance, authentic wooden lamps featured on each
table and background music offered the tranquil
strains of flutes and tinkling bells.

Settling in, Libby set her bag aside. 'You enjoy
your stays in Malaysia?'

'I don't usually see much outside of Sepang.
That's the town and district where the race is held
each year. It's a hop from the international airport
to the circuit.'

Alex sat back while a waiter, who had already
seen to the placement of Libby's linen napkin, now
laid a starched white square on the gentleman's lap.
As Libby took in the surrounds and her compel-
ling company, a thought struck her. This was the

first time she'd been with Alex in public and she sensed others in the room absorbing and reacting to his appealing air of authority too.

Was it that some people in the restaurant, including the waiter, recognised Alex out of his racing gear? Or was it as she suspected? That no matter where he might be, Alex Wolfe radiated a presence that commanded attention. Even deference.

As the waiter moved off, Alex continued. 'I plan to visit Malaysia purely for a vacation one day.'

'Ever get tired of living out of a suitcase?' she asked, feeling the beat of her pulse increase at the way his big tanned hand brushed the white table-cloth. His eyes searched hers and he considered her words.

'That's an interesting question coming from one who would know about such things.'

A wistful feeling drifted through her. She didn't think often of those days, travelling the world over for her sport. Better to concentrate on the blessings she'd kept and new opportunities she'd created. But she could easily admit, 'I loved the travel. Around Australia as much as around the world.'

His grey eyes glittered. 'Your favourite port?'

'Brazil is awesome. Malibu for the nostalgia. But…Maui.' Remembering the thrill of riding those two and a half metre barrels, she smiled. 'Yeah. Definitely Maui.'

'Sounds as if you were Australia's answer to *Gidget*.'

She smiled at the connection. 'A lot of people don't realise the girl from that old movie and series was based on a real person.'

'The first female world champion?'

'*Gidget* was written in the fifties.' Libby still owned the copy she'd picked up at a second-hand store the summer she'd turned thirteen. 'The first female championship wasn't until 1964. Won by a Sydneyite,' she noted with pride. 'She was awarded two hundred and fifty dollars, a new surfboard and several packets of cigarettes.'

He laughed, an easy sound that made Libby feel as if they'd known each other for years. 'The things you learn on a date with your physio.'

Libby's smile fell at the same time her heart rolled over. This wasn't a *date*. This was lunch with a client. A handsome client with incredibly strong features and soft grey eyes that seemed to be inviting her in.

Shifting in her chair, Libby collected her food menu, although she suddenly felt so flustered she couldn't concentrate on the words.

Alex collected his menu too, and after a time commented, 'I rang my brother.'

Her gaze shot up and menu went down. 'Jacob?'

'Think I told you we haven't seen each other since he left all those years ago.'

'That must have been hard. Your oldest brother leaving without a word.'

'I don't think he had any option.'

When he beckoned the waiter over, Libby leaned forward. Elbows on the table, she laced her fingers and rested her chin on the bridge. After that day in his amazing garage when she'd learned Alex knew of her surfing history, she'd been taken so off guard, had felt so undercut, she vowed never to talk personal again. And she'd stuck to that.

But so what if the fact she'd had an accident happened to come up? It would make no difference to her attitude or commitment to their sessions, and shouldn't she give Alex the benefit of the doubt that he would still value her abilities as a physio? As a human being?

And what harm could come from hearing more about the mysterious Wolfe clan? In truth, she was beyond intrigued. A father nobody missed. A brother who'd escaped in the dead of night. Eight siblings in all, one of whom was Alex's twin, the sister who'd contacted him before his terrible crash.

After Alex ordered a bottle of cabernet sauvignon, Libby said, 'You and your brother must have had a lot to talk about.'

'It was a little awkward speaking again after so many years. I was only fourteen when Jacob left. But we'd always got along.'

He wove a fingertip aimlessly over the pearl etched on the menu, perhaps wondering if he ought to divulge anything more. For a moment she thought she glimpsed pain lurking in the shadows of his gaze and words of support rose up. Yes, she was curious but they could talk about something else if the past hurt too much to discuss. She understood, more than he might ever know.

But then he swept up his water glass, took a sip and met her gaze again.

'Wolfe Manor has been declared structurally unsafe and a danger to the community,' he said. 'Jacob wants to repair the damage. No easy feat.'

Repair the damage...Libby had the feeling Alex was speaking about more than fixing some dilapidated ancient house.

'Does Jacob think it's salvageable?'

'Rising damp, holes in the roof, crumbling brick, grounds grown wild. Vandals did a number on it too. But apparently Jacob's an architect now. He plans to refurbish the manor completely, then sell it on.' His jaw tightening, Alex seemed to look inward. 'Frankly, I can't see how he can set foot in that place again.' His gaze cleared as it darted over her shoulder and his chin kicked up. 'Here comes the wine.'

As the waiter presented the label for Alex to acknowledge, Libby pressed her lips together. These weeks she'd tried to keep a professional distance between herself and Alex. He was the kind of man any woman could get distracted by. And in only a few moments of conversation, she was looking at him not as a client or even a world-renowned top athlete but a real person, with regrets and fears as well as the courage to overcome them.

She wanted to hear more about the ghosts that seemed to inhabit Wolfe Manor. She imagined streams of cobwebs, fallen-down stairs, skeletons in every closet. But how much more was Alex prepared to divulge?

Wine poured, Alex raised his glass. 'Here's to my speedy recovery.'

'Here's to a healthy future.'

He grinned over the rim of his glass and sipped.

'What other news did your bother have?' she asked, savouring the wine's oaky flavour while lowering her glass.

'Now this is interesting.' When he tipped forward, his shoulders seemed to grow as the space between them closed. Libby's nerve endings began to hum. Thank heaven they would never kiss. She might go up in flames!

'Another brother, Lucas, is involved with Hartington's.'

'The big UK store?'

Alex nodded. 'The venue which was supposed to host the company's centennial party pulled out at the last minute and Lucas ended up hosting the bash on the Wolfe Manor grounds. The place was apparently surrounded by scaffolds, but they'd restored a good portion of the lawns to their former aristocratic glory. Another brother, Nathaniel, was there on the night.'

Libby's mind wound back. That Christian name gelled with Alex's surname and then exploded in her head.

'Not Nathaniel Wolfe the actor? The movie star who won that big award a couple of months ago?'

'One and the same. There was a scandal surrounding his West End debut.'

'I read about it.'

'He hid away on a privately owned island off the coast of South America.'

'Nathaniel owns an island?'

'No. Another brother, Sebastian.'

Near overwhelmed, Libby blew out a breath. 'The Wolfe kids did well for themselves.'

'Despite all odds.'

Again Libby saw that shadow darken his gaze, drag on his mouth, and she shivered. Just how bad had his childhood been?

'Anyway,' he went on easily, pretending to himself that his past didn't worry him when it was obvious that it did, 'seems Nathaniel fell in love with the woman he kidnapped—'

She frowned. 'Oh, now you're making it up.'

He raised a hand—Scout's honour. 'And at this centennial night they announced their plans to marry.'

Emotion flooded her throat and a mist came over her eyes. Silly to have such a strong emotion, but that evening sounded like a fabulous fairytale ending. One any girl might dream of. *If* she were ready for that kind of thing. If she'd found the right one.

'I hope they'll be very happy,' Libby said with the utmost sincerity. 'Are you invited to the wedding?'

'I have a previous engagement.'

Questioning, she angled her head and realised he was talking about a race. But she didn't want to put a damper on their conversation, ask about dates and then get into the old 'you might not be fit to drive' argument. Today she didn't want to discuss that at all.

The waiter appeared, refilled their near-empty glasses and enquired, 'Are you ready to order, sir?'

'Five minutes,' Alex replied, and pulled a mock guilty face as the waiter walked away. 'Guess we ought to make some decisions.'

Libby glanced at her watch and gasped. 'Where's the time gone?'

'Seems you won't make it back to the office in an hour.'

'That speech won't go away.'

'Precisely. It'll be there tomorrow. So let's enjoy what's left of today.'

When he raised his glass, she hesitated but then lifted hers too. Just this once, who said life had to be all work and no play?

CHAPTER SIX

HE AND Libby took their time with their meals, savouring the exotic flavours and brilliant bay views. A dessert wine was ordered to go with pineapple tarts to end off. Now as the waiter took the empty dessert dishes, Alex moved to fill his companion's glass again, but Libby held up both hands.

'Thank you, but I've had more than enough.'

'You're not still pretending that you're going back to work,' he chided.

'But it's only—' She checked her watch, then, amazed, glanced around the near-deserted restaurant. 'Four o'clock?'

Alex smiled. He hadn't known hours could melt away so quickly either.

Libby was a different person away from her work—not cool or reserved at all. They'd talked about the places they'd travelled. The different aspects of their chosen sports. He'd learned more about her background, growing up on Sydney beaches with parents who cared about her and her dreams. Even now he couldn't imagine what it must be like to be the product of a happy home. Made him wonder for the first time about being a parent himself.

What kind of father would he make? Would he be overly protective because of his unhappy history or would the shadow of William Wolfe try to descend upon and direct him as it once had his older brother?

During their recent phone conversation, Jacob had opened up. He'd explained how he'd become increasingly agitated after the court case involving the death of their father and had jumped down poor Annabelle's throat that last day he'd spent at Wolfe Manor twenty years ago. Jacob had been afraid that if he stayed, he'd become the monster their father had been.

If Alex had been Jacob, he'd have run too. Better than filling his siblings, who had looked up to their oldest brother, with loathing and fear. He supposed they all had their crosses to bear, scars from their childhood at Wolfe Manor, but perhaps none more than Annabelle. While Jacob had been there to save her that dark night, Alex had been the brother who had unintentionally sent his beautiful twin to face a horrible fate. It was all so many years ago and yet lately the memories had become more vivid. Harder to escape or play down.

Clearly because he had too much time on his hands.

With renewed energy, he set the bottle back in its ice bucket. 'What say you give me a lesson?'

Libby was folding her napkin. 'Lesson?'

'Surfing.' He cupped his right shoulder. 'Might be just what the ol' boy needs.'

She held his gaze before pushing her folded napkin away. 'There's lots of professionals who teach for a living.'

'I was thinking more for fun.'

A diversion. Like today.

She sent a mild censuring look. 'We'll stick to our regular exercises.'

He persisted. 'After listening to your surf tales, I'm obviously missing something pretty special.'

And he couldn't think of anyone he'd rather have teach him. He couldn't think of anyone he'd rather see in a bikini. Or out of one, for that matter.

Although he understood Libby's attire during their sessions was meant to match her professional demeanour, those long white drawstring pants she wore weren't terribly flattering. Once in a while a sensible pair of shorts wouldn't hurt; a not so sensible pair wouldn't either. Unfortunately he couldn't see a change of wardrobe during work hours. Which meant he'd need to suggest some outing that would invite a less...*restricted* look.

Yes. He wanted to see more of Libby and, after

today, he believed she'd like to see more of him. Most importantly, this spending time outside of work-related matters had eased his mind about China. The open, supportive Libby he'd come to know today wouldn't hold him back. And rather than pushing his point and possibly getting her back up, now he thought it wiser to simply keep her onside. When the time came, just as she'd accepted today's invitation to lunch, she would also give his shoulder an early checkmark.

After signing the bill, Alex escorted his lunch date outside. They passed a wall displaying the restaurant's logo—a shimmering pearl bedded in a clamshell.

'If you were known as a mermaid,' he said, his palm coming to rest against her lower back, 'I'm betting pearls are your bling of choice.'

As she'd done earlier, she wound away from his touch. 'I'm not so much into jewellery.'

He cast a doubtful look. 'I thought every woman was into diamonds, at least.'

'Not this woman.'

Her smile was almost tight, which, after such a relaxing lunch, made him wonder.

Obviously she thought she needed to explain. 'It's not that I don't think gems are pretty. As a matter of fact, I think pearls are beautiful. I just don't own any. I'm more of a practical type.' She held up her wrist. 'I own a watch.'

Examining the piece, he frowned to himself. A sports dial, not at all feminine. He supposed some females weren't into rings and things. Or would Libby be flattered, like most women, to be given a stunning necklace, bracelet or something even more special?

As they slid into the limo, Alex stole a glance at his companion's hands while she excused herself to check her mobile for messages. Those fingers had been on display practically every day for two weeks. He'd known she wasn't engaged. That had come out in Eli's initial research. But was she seeing anyone on a more casual basis?

When his gut kicked, he scrubbed his jaw.

Well, why wouldn't she be? She was an extremely attractive, highly intelligent woman with a great deal to offer a man. And if she were indeed seeing someone, her usual 'I'm only about work' demeanour—the way she avoided his casual touch—made more sense. As for accepting his invitation to lunch today… An important client showing up out the blue? He hadn't given her much choice.

He swallowed a curse.

Just when he'd felt better about this whole situation. But the day wasn't over yet. Still time to find out more.

'It's going on four-thirty,' he said, when she slid her phone away. 'Too late to go back to the office.

And you can't drive after the wine. I'll drop you home.'

Libby gazed off, no doubt considering her options. Clearly seeing the merit in his suggestion, she nodded and gave the driver her address, which was less than five minutes away. When the limo pulled up, Alex swung out, then helped her onto the footpath. With an almost shy smile, she looped her bag more securely over a shoulder.

'Lunch was a lovely surprise. Thank you.'

'I'll see you to the entrance.'

Other than her pupils dilating, her expression remained unaffected. 'There's really no need.'

'You'll offend my sense of chivalry.'

She blinked as though she wasn't sure if he were joking. While he kept a straight face—he *always* walked his dates to their doors—she thought it through, finally gave in to a shadow of a smile and walked alongside him toward her building. Once they reached the glass security door, however, she pulled up to her full height and faced him.

End of the line.

'Well, here we are and, uh—' she peered around him '—your driver's waiting.'

'That's what I pay him for,' he said. 'Driving and waiting.'

Done with pretext, she eased out a breath. 'I know what you're thinking. We've had a nice few hours and you'd like me to invite you up.' She shook her head. 'Not a good idea.'

'I disagree.'

Her amber eyes flared. 'Neither of us want this to get complicated.'

'Who said it has to be complicated?'

Growing more nervous, she wet her lips. 'We have a working relationship we need to maintain.'

'This is working for me.' He stepped closer and his head lowered, close to hers. 'How about you?'

He hadn't set out to kiss her, but his mouth found hers, nevertheless. Then he told himself to keep it light, no more than a lingering brush of his lips over hers. But as they touched, an overwhelming need to explore broke through and instinctively his hands found her shoulders and winged them gently in.

White heat unfurled high on each thigh as the heavy beat of his heart echoed through his veins. He urged her nearer, until her breasts pressed low against his chest and, as he kneaded her flesh, the tight beads pushing against her blouse rubbed and hardened more. His tongue ran over her teeth and when her mouth opened wider, inviting him in as she dissolved, Alex forgot they were in public, in broad daylight, doing what should be enjoyed behind the privacy of closed doors. He forgot everything except the wonderful way Libby felt in his arms and his desire to know more.

He was taken off guard when her palms spliced up between them and, groaning, she pushed away. Short on breath, Libby avoided his gaze as she flattened a hand against the entry door to steady herself. 'Why did you do that?'

'You have to ask?'

Other than the deep rise and fall of her chest, she didn't move. Her cheeks scorched red, she merely lifted her gaze and glared at him. 'Alex, don't *ever* do that again.'

'Because you're my physio?'

Pressing her glistening lips together, she nodded deeply. 'Exactly. And…' She rose up a little. 'I'm not after a relationship right now.'

He smiled softly. 'That's a shame.'

A flame leapt in her eyes and for a moment he thought she might reconsider and ask him up but then she punched a number into the security pad and, in a blink, disappeared inside.

On his way back to the limo, Alex went over every second of that delectable kiss as well as the steps which had led him to this unique point in time. He'd gone from admitting that Libby Henderson had grown on him to openly confessing he wanted to broaden the scope on their relationship. This morning he'd merely wanted to get to the bottom of what lay behind her ice queen act, as well as confirm that she was still onside with regard to his plans for China. And yet now he found himself enjoying a woman's company like he never had before. Hell, he'd even winced at a spike of jealousy when he'd thought of Libby with another man.

Not good.

Standing guard by the limo, the driver opened the back passenger's door. Rubbing the back of his neck, Alex climbed inside.

He couldn't remember being rejected by a lady since tenth grade. Hands down it wouldn't matter so much if it weren't this particular one, because the bald-faced truth was that Libby had done *more* than grow on him. She'd burrowed under his skin. Was playing more and more on his mind. And that was a condition he was less than happy to entertain; he had enough on his mind as it was.

He needed to avoid unnecessary complications. Ipso facto, this state of affairs had to cease and desist. If Libby wasn't interested in having him hold her, getting involved, as of this moment that went double for him.

CHAPTER SEVEN

THE next morning, Libby strode into that lavish Rose Bay home with her head down and nothing but work on her mind. Or that's what she needed Alex Wolfe to believe.

He'd caught her unawares yesterday afternoon. After their lunch, she'd known he was hinting at an invitation upstairs into her apartment, but when she'd knocked him back she'd never expected him to *kiss* her. And what a kiss! For one dizzy moment, she'd almost reconsidered and dragged him inside. But then all those old fears had come creeping back in.

Although they'd had a better than good physical relationship, after her accident Scott hadn't wanted to be around, let alone *touch*, her. She'd thought Scott was the one, but when she'd needed him most—needed to know she could still be desirable—he'd not only let her down, he'd left her with a huge question mark hanging over her head. She hated to be a glass-half-full type and yet there were times when she couldn't help but wonder…

What man wouldn't view her the same way Scott had?

Although she felt Alex's eyes simmering over her now as she moved off in front and down that long hall, she kept her demeanour neutral and, as she'd done every day for the preceding two weeks, set her bag down in its usual place in the gym. Despite her bravado, she felt the telltale signs of his close proximity already at work on her. Fluttering heartbeat. Elevated breathing pattern. The effervescent buzz her blood acquired simply knowing he was near. Those reactions had been bad enough in the past, particularly whenever her skin touched his. But after that heart-stopping kiss…

Libby's mind froze.

Would he try to kiss her again?

'How are you feeling this morning?'

On her way past a treadmill, Libby's step faltered. That was *her* usual pre-session question to Alex, not the other way round.

'Fine,' she replied, without meeting his gaze.

'I've already done some work on my shoulder this morning,' he told her in a level tone that suggested he wasn't comfortable with her being here today. Which answered her question about whether he might try to kiss her again.

Well, if he felt uncomfortable, she thought,

taking up her position before the mirror, he had only himself to blame. If her rejection had stung, maybe he ought to join the rest of humanity and toughen up.

'Let's see where we are with your range of motion.' She felt his eyes on her reflection but she kept her focus on his shoulder and her mind on work. Finally, brooding, he wound out of his shirt and she instructed, 'Arms out front, please.'

As if his soles were lined with lead, he angled toward the mirror, braced his legs and both arms gradually went out.

'Raise them slowly,' she said.

She stole a glance at his expression. His unshaven jaw was drawn tight and his gaze was distant and stormy. If he wanted to make this morning more difficult than it needed to be, he could do his worst. As far as she was concerned—and, it seemed, he too—yesterday's indiscretions were behind them. Doubly good because now she didn't need to ponder over how Alex might behave if he discovered she wasn't all he presumed.

Alex was already lowering his arms but she noted he hadn't lifted them as high as he had been. Not anywhere near.

She moved to stand in front. 'Again, please.'

A muscle beat in the tight angle of that jaw, then he raised both arms again to that same point he had the first time. When he let them drop as if he couldn't be bothered, he moved to sweep up the shirt he'd cast off.

'That's it for today,' he told her. 'I'm done.'

Her physio antennae tingling, Libby followed as he marched off. He wasn't hiding anything. She'd caught his wince before he'd lowered his arms.

'Your shoulder hurts?' Knowing the answer, she went on. 'Describe the pain.'

He eased his right arm through its sleeve. 'It's nothing.'

'You said you'd already worked out this morning.' She crossed to her bag, retrieved her apricot kernel oil and moved to the massage table. 'Can you come over here and lie down?' She added over her shoulder, 'Shirt off again, please.'

'Libby, I don't want a massage.'

She tried to ignore the ripple of frustration in his tone. Whether this morning was awkward was inconsequential. He'd overdone his exercises and a remedial massage was the right call. If he wanted to get back on track, he'd best suck it up and do as he was told.

'Sounds as if you've overexerted the muscles,' she said. 'I'm going to work over the accumulation of trigger points—those painful knots—that are restricting your range of movement.' His chin down, he exhaled and continued to glare the other way. She fisted her hands on her hips. 'Do you want to get back as soon as possible or don't you?'

His penetrating gaze hooked back onto hers at the same time his palm slid up his right arm. She wondered if his ego was dented enough that he might be done with it and order her out. But then he shrugged back out of his shirt and joined her.

Her stomach muscles squeezed like they did whenever he was near—particularly when he was half naked—but she clicked her mind onto professional mode, uncapped the oil and arranged some towels, which were laid on a tray near the table.

'Spread out,' she said. He hoisted himself up and lay down. 'Now just relax and we'll have those muscles loosened up in no time.'

Starting lightly, she kneaded the area to warm up the tissue. After finding several trigger points, she used her thumbs and fingers to press and manipulate, gradually applying more and more pressure. Five minutes in, when she began to drill a particularly stubborn knot, he jumped.

'*Aahh!* You're a bit vigorous there, doc.'

'Stay with me,' she said. 'We'll work out these problems, then you'll need to drop down your exercises for a few days and start back with lower repetitions.'

'I don't have that time.'

Setting her jaw, she stopped rubbing. *Enough.*

'If you'd prefer, I can help you find someone else.'

Dammit, she knew what she was doing and he

could either work with her or find another physio. She was over the tiptoe show, on every level. It was difficult but if she could control her inappropriate feelings toward him, surely Alex could shelf his as well.

The tension locking his scapulas loosened. He faced the sheet once again and muttered, 'Do what you have to.'

Half satisfied, Libby applied more oil and soon she was in the zone again, doing what she did best—letting her fingers work their magic, giving a client's impaired muscles new life.

Alex lay on that table like a good patient, gritting his teeth as Libby kneaded and rubbed and slid her hands over his apricot-scented knot-infested back. When she hit a spot that shot a hot bolt screaming through to his chest, this time he curled his toes and bit off the groan. He and remedial massages weren't strangers but he could tell *this* technique was truly hitting the mark. Not only that. The touching and rocking was also expelling barrel loads of all kinds of endorphins. Given he'd decided it wiser not to pursue those feelings where Libby was concerned, this was not a good thing.

For Libby's part, he knew this time was strictly about his shoulder. Nothing lay behind her tactile attentions other than her need to do the best she could for his recovering injury and rectify the setback he had brought about; trying to work Libby and memories of that kiss out of his system, he'd pushed himself too hard with the bands this morning. From *his* current position, however—a purely male point of view—her organic manipulations were working more than one kind of wonder.

He and Libby had touched before. Yesterday when they'd embraced, he'd dwelled on how good it would feel to experience more. Now, through this ultra hands-on method, he'd got a big insight into that and the buzz was having its effects in places he couldn't control.

'How does that feel?' she asked.

Eyes closed, he sighed. To be honest? 'Fabulous.'

Her palm gave one last glorious sweep of his warmed skin. 'Make sure you rest over the weekend.'

Frowning, he cracked open one eye. It was over?

'You can't leave yet.' He groaned, groggy—aroused—then, knowing insistence wouldn't work, he appealed to her professional sense of compassion. 'There's still a twinge in my traps.'

Her brows jumped. 'Oh?'

She inspected the area, shook out more oil and then her hands were working over his back again and that delicious buzz circulating through his system grew stronger. Burned brighter.

After a few moments, she asked, 'Does that feel better?'

With his cheek rubbing against the sheet, he hummed out a smile. 'Definitely.'

When her fingers lingered, then trailed slowly away, he wondered if a smidgeon of private pleasure had leaked into her professional sphere as well. After that kiss he didn't buy that she wasn't interested in him in a XY kind of way. He was close to certain she wouldn't stymie his return to the track earlier than Morrissey had subscribed. Therefore he didn't need to worry about building up more of a rapport…doing what he could to make certain she was on his side. In fact, he'd decided trying to push the intimacy point now might prove detrimental to his primary goal.

Better for everyone concerned if he simply backed off, no matter how his current testosterone levels might object.

She left off to wipe her hands. 'All the bumps are gone now,' she said.

That wasn't entirely true, he thought as he pushed up and gingerly swung his legs over the table's side. Beneath his shorts, his erection was of the opinion that all this rubbing was deeply personal. Grabbing a towel off the tray, he let its tail hang and cover the front of his shorts as he fake-rubbed his chest.

'Drink plenty of water.' Recapping her oil, she gave a practiced smile. 'I'll see you Monday.'

As she crossed to her bag, still holding his towel, he edged off the table. No question, he should let her be on her way. Then maybe he could call up a few friends, organise a weekend in Paris or Milan. Anywhere away from here. All this tension... He merely needed to shake loose and get out.

So what was stopping him?

He took two steps toward her, stopped, then, driven, took another.

'About yesterday...' he began.

'It's in the past. There's nothing to say.' She stuffed the plastic bottle away and lobbed the bag over her shoulder.

He exhaled. Absently rubbed his chest again. She was right. He even said it aloud.

'You're right.'

'Remember, take a rest until I see you next.'

Clutching that towel, he walked forward to see her out. 'I won't lift a single weight,' he confirmed. 'I won't even think of this room.'

I definitely won't think of you.

Her brow slowly creased; she'd noticed him advancing and took a step back. 'I can see myself out.'

'If you prefer. There's just one thing.'

'What's that?'

'What happened…' His hand fisted in the towel before he tossed it aside. 'It's not in the past.'

Her eyes rounded with alarm. 'Alex, you agreed. There's nothing more to say.'

'Correct. I'm all done talking.'

With his good arm, he reached and drew her near. He saw her eyes flare and knew a moment when she might have told him to back off and let her be. But then the breath seemed to leave her body, her lids grew heavy and he saw her heart glistening there in her eyes. He was right. This situation—this maddening push and pull—couldn't go on. Now was the time to end it. And end it his way.

Even as Alex's head slanted over hers and Libby drifted off into the caress, some weak, desperate part of her cried out that this should not, *could* not, happen. But as the kiss deepened and her head grew light, eventually she forgot the reasons why. The slow velvet slide of his tongue over hers, the way his hands pressed her gloriously near…she could only wonder at the amount of strength it had taken yesterday to tear herself away.

This may be dangerous, but it felt so infinitely right. This minute she only knew she was absorbed by sensation. Absorbed, and lifted up, by him.

Her palms ironed up over his bare hot chest at the same time his hands pressed down over her back. His head angled as he curled over her, his touch sculpting her behind, hooking around her thigh and urging it to curl around his hip as his pelvis locked with hers. She felt the perspiration building on his skin, the glide of his hand scrooping around her thigh, sliding lower toward her knee—

Breathless—terrified—she yanked away.

Oh, God, she'd vowed this wouldn't happen again.

She didn't want him to know.

'This is a working relationship,' she grated out, trembling.

'Who says it can't be more?'

Alex gathered her in and the next she knew they were kissing again, and this time he wasn't playing. Now he delivered his full punch, and the effects left her reeling, helpless. Giddy. He whipped up a hurricane inside of her, a dark powerful storm that tossed her off course and hurled her places that promised such blissful satisfaction. But the edges of her mind were still calling. As much as she might want to—and she wanted to so badly— she couldn't go through with any of this.

This time when she broke the kiss, their lips remained close. She couldn't get enough air. Couldn't stop the hot flood of emotion.

'You don't…don't understand.'

His brow furrowed and eyes turned dark. He

shook his head. 'No, Libby, I'm afraid I don't.' He searched her eyes. 'Has someone hurt you?'

She wanted to tell him everything. Say, yes, as a matter of fact she *had* been hurt and deeply. She'd had a wonderful life, what she thought had been a wonderful fiancé, then the world had crashed in and she hadn't been with a man since. When Scott had rejected her—when his tight expression had told her the thought of touching her repelled him—it had left scars that made her leg injury seem like a scratch.

Alex's gaze pierced hers as a different light flashed in his eyes. 'Are you seeing someone else?'

As if.

'The point is, Alex, I didn't sign up for this.'

'Sometimes life throws us a curve ball.'

She coughed out a humourless laugh. 'Thanks for the tip.'

He studied her and finally blew out a long defeated breath. He even slid a foot back. 'Look, what if we calm down and give each other a break?'

'I like that idea. On one condition.' She implored him with her eyes. 'You don't ever try to touch me again.'

As Libby walked out, Alex's every muscle clenched, ready to leap and drag her back. Because he didn't believe her. She *wanted* him to hold her again. Kiss her again. What the hell was stopping her?

He tried to put himself in her shoes. Seemed her job meant everything to her, as much as his career meant to him. She didn't want to jeopardise her reputation or professional integrity by becoming intimately involved with a client who had made no secret of his need to attain an early checkmark for his shoulder.

But her need to avoid him went deeper than that.

Imagining her marching out his front door, Alex strode in the opposite direction, down toward the rowers, then he strode back and, fuelled by frustration, kicked a treadmill, and kicked it again. He hadn't felt this keyed up since he was a kid with no good way to expend his energy. But huffing around and fracturing his foot wouldn't help. Learning more about Libby might.

His mobile sat on the ledge outside the sauna. He snapped it up. When Eli answered, he got to the point. 'What else do you know about Libby Henderson?'

Silence echoed down the line before Eli replied, 'What's wrong? She's not doing her job?'

'Eli, I'll give you three seconds. What else do you know?'

Eli blew out a long breath before he began to talk, and as he explained and the pieces fell into place, Alex sank lower and lower until he was sitting, gobsmacked, on the floor. He cursed under his breath. Tried to shake off the tingles racing over his skin. He'd had no idea. Not a bloody clue. But now when he thought about Libby's cool facade, about the way she'd literally jumped out of her skin today when he'd reached for her leg…

His gut twisted and his head dropped to his knees.

How did you tell someone something like that? He'd never told anyone about *his* deepest wounds… the hurts, and shame, he pushed aside every day.

'Alex? You there?'

His stomach churning, Alex lifted his head. He felt wrung out, as if he'd spent a day behind the wheel navigating the toughest track on the circuit.

'Yeah,' he groaned, holding his brow. 'I'm here.'

'I'll come over.'

'*No.* I'm fine.'

'It shouldn't make a difference—'

'You're wrong, Eli,' he cut in. 'It makes a difference.' Then he asked the obvious. 'Why didn't you tell me?'

'Because you didn't need to know.'

Alex let go the breath he'd been holding. His friend was right. He hadn't needed to know about Libby's accident. When he'd hired her, those kinds of personal details were none of his business. Now...

He pushed to his feet.

That detail changed everything.

CHAPTER EIGHT

AFTER a very unsettling day that had started in the most unsettling way, Libby let herself into her apartment. Dropping everything, she filled the tub, peeled off her clothes, then sank into the wonderful warm suds. Her head resting against a vinyl pillow, she closed her eyes and sighed. She felt drained. Confused.

What was she supposed to do now?

This morning, despite her best efforts to avoid another incident, Alex had kissed her soundly again, and for a second time she'd kissed him back. Even now her cheeks burned remembering how easily she'd succumbed. Worse, despite ultimately turning her back and walking away, a silly self-destructive part of her couldn't help but wish he would take her in his arms again. One dose of Alex Wolfe had been bad enough. Now that she'd tasted him twice, she was in grave danger of becoming addicted.

After Scott, she'd let herself get close to only

one man. Leo Tamms had gone to her university, majored in civil engineering and had asked her out three times. She thought they'd got on well. On their last date, they'd even kissed goodnight. One day in the cafeteria he'd asked why she walked with a limp—she hadn't perfected her gait back then. In his eyes she could see Leo suspected anyway, so she'd garnered her strength and told him her story. Leo had seemed interested, sympathetic, but he hadn't asked her out again. In fact, whenever he saw her coming, he slipped a one-eighty and streaked the other way.

That episode had hurt almost as much as Scott's rejection. It confirmed the doubt that had lurked at the back of her mind since the accident—that many people were shallow enough to judge others by their wrapping rather than what they really offered, which was underneath. Was Alex Wolfe one of those people?

Twenty minutes later, feeling more relaxed, Libby dried off. Tying the ribbon sash of her floor-length negligee, she moved into the kitchen, opened the fridge and eyed some leftover chicken stir-fry. But her appetite had been MIA all day. Her stomach was too full of butterflies with her wondering what would come next in this ill-fated game Alex seemed intent on playing. So she poured a glass of milk to line her stomach and, sipping, crossed into the living room.

She could work on that speech, she supposed, or put on a movie, read a book. Or sit here all night wishing life weren't so complicated. She'd been content before Alex Wolfe had inserted himself into her life. She'd been at peace with herself and what she'd accomplished. Now it seemed she was weighed down with questions. Sometimes, like at lunch yesterday, she could almost convince herself that Alex was sincerely interested in her. But common sense said he was far more interested in how he could use her…what she could give: a free pass to China.

When the building entrance buzzer sounded, Libby stiffened. But then she siphoned down some air and got a grip. Her imagination would be the death of her. Of course it wasn't Alex Wolfe buzzing. It was a friend dropped by. Or a delivery of some kind.

Chiding herself, she headed for the intercom, thumbed a button and said hello. The voice that resonated back was deep and hauntingly familiar.

'I hoped I'd find you home.'

Libby held her stomach as her midsection double clutched and a lump of anxiety lodged in her throat. She took one shaky step back and clapped shut her hanging jaw. Then she got her thoughts and courage together and, resolute, leaned toward the speaker.

'What are you doing here?'

'I brought you something.'

She frowned. Brought her what exactly? But she didn't want to know. He needed to leave.

He needed to leave *now*.

'You can give me whatever it is on Monday.'

'It might be dead by then.'

She stopped to think. Did he say *dead*?

His voice lowered. 'Please, Libby, let me up.'

She hugged herself as her stomach looped again and her thoughts scurried on. She ought to tell him to get in his limo, if that's how he'd got here, and cruise straight back to his palatial home. God knows she didn't need this aggravation.

The intercom crackled. 'Libby, I need to apologise for today.'

Her chest twisted and she screwed her eyes shut. She raised her voice. 'Go away.'

'Five minutes, then I promise to leave.'

Feeling ill, she bowed over. She didn't want to let him in. But then she wanted to so much. More to the point, Alex's mind seemed set. He wanted to apologise in person for his behaviour this morning and instinct warned her that he wouldn't leave until he did. That kind of one-eyed determination was a big part of the reason he was a World Number One.

Groaning, she hit the entry button, then retrieved a wrap from her wardrobe to cover her negligee. By the time she made it back, a knock was sounding on her door. After driving her damp palms down her sides, for better or worse, she reached for the handle and prepared to open up.

Alex waited outside the apartment door, clearing his throat, rocking on his heels, more nervous than he'd been in a long time. Since Eli had revealed Libby's secret earlier today, he'd thought of nothing but. The fact he'd seen her only in those long white pants, the way she wove away if ever he got too close…now it all made sense.

His interest in her had started out as purely mercenary. He'd been determined to do what was necessary to keep his pretty physio onside and willing to sign off early on his injury. But even before this week's lunch date, he'd begun to see Libby Henderson differently. After that first kiss—the way she'd cut him off and strode away—he'd told himself no matter how much she intrigued him, it would be wiser to play the attraction down and forget that caress had ever happened.

Not possible.

This morning he'd kissed her again. After the initial merging of mouths and climbing of heat, she had broken away and served up an even frostier dismissal. *Don't ever try to touch me again.*

He couldn't do that.

Shifting his weight, he told his jangling nerves to quieten at the same time he looked down to inspect what he'd brought. A way to break the ice, get them talking. Hopefully get beyond this impasse.

God, he hoped she liked it.

Libby fanned open the door to find Alex standing on her threshold, looking as amazing as he had the other day when he'd appeared at her office out of nowhere. But tonight the sight of his tall broad-shouldered frame was beyond overwhelming. That slanted smile became more alluring— more tempting—every time they met.

Stepping closer, he held out his gift. 'This is for you.'

Her gaze dropped and, perplexed, she lifted one shoulder and let it drop. 'You're giving me a stick of bamboo?'

'It's a peace offering.'

'An unusual one,' she decided, accepting the stick. Then she noticed a fan of delicate flowers hanging from a shoot.

'Most bamboo only flower once every few decades.'

Really? 'I didn't know that.'

'It has deep symbolic meaning in Asian countries.'

Understanding the connection, she half grinned. 'You mean like Malaysia.'

'There they speak of a legend where a man

dreams of a beautiful woman while he sleeps under a bamboo plant. When he wakes, he breaks the bamboo stem and discovers that the woman is inside.'

Libby's heart beat high in her throat. Was he in some way comparing the couple in the legend to them? Gathering herself, she cleared her throat.

'That's a lovely story.'

'An old man in Sepang once told me that bamboo bends in a storm—' he took the top of the stem she now held and slanted it to the left '—and when the storm is over it stands straight again.' He set it right. 'It never loses its original ground...its integrity.'

She held her breath against a push of emotion. Now he was definitely talking about her...telling her that bending here, now, with him, wouldn't affect the respect she'd earned in her profession. He'd gone to a lot of trouble—finding this flowering piece of bamboo, looking into legends and symbols of the East. She was touched, and yet the voice of caution implored her to beware.

'Alex, why are you here?'

His gaze lingered over her lips and his voice dropped to that deep drawl that sent her heart pounding and common sense melting into a puddle.

'You know why I'm here.'

When his hand slid down the stem and covered

hers, his skin on hers felt so good. In a strange way, familiar. Two minutes together, one small touch, and already she felt about to crumple.

But then she bit her lip and shook her head. She wanted to believe what she felt when they'd kissed was real. She wanted to be like so many other women who took a chance and were willing to see where things led. But she couldn't take the next step.

She was frightened to.

She lifted her chin. 'This shouldn't happen. We shouldn't get involved.'

The back of his free hand brushed her cheek. 'Too late.'

She was shaking inside and when his head lowered and his mouth skimmed her brow, overcome with deepest longing, she quivered to her toes.

Against her hair, he murmured, 'Say you're not angry with me.'

When his lips grazed her temple and his warm breath brushed her ear, torn in two, she groaned. 'I'm angrier with myself.'

'Let it go,' he told her.

And then she was lost in his kiss, a caress more beautiful, more erotic, than any she'd known. Perhaps because this time she'd almost surrendered. Almost submitted to what seemed inevitable. But was this what she wanted? Did she need to open up this much to a man she'd known only two weeks? Even if he seemed so sincere?

Needing air—needing *space*—she broke away and held her forehead.

'Alex, you're confusing me.'

'I'm trying to be clear.'

His hands wound around her waist and his mouth claimed hers again. But she wanted to explain…needed to let him know…

The rest of that thought evaporated when reality ceased to exist and both her arms floated up to coil around his neck. His chest rumbled with satisfaction and she felt his smile as she liquefied like a dollop of creamy butter in the sun. But as his palm slid down over her hip, then her thigh, a sliver of reason shone through the drugging fog. If she truly intended to go through with this—make love—there was something he needed to know.

Reluctantly this time she drew away. His breathing heavy, he rested his brow against hers and smiled into her eyes. 'You're not going to say you're still confused.'

'There's something I need to tell you.'

His lips nipped hers as he brought her gently flush against his body. 'You don't need to tell me anything.'

Her stomach pitched. 'I really do.'

Stepping back, she caught her skirts and began

to ease the satin up. But Alex kept his eyes on hers.

'Libby...I know.'

Her hands curled more tightly into the satin and, as her throat thickened, she frowned.

'You...know?' *About my accident? About my leg?* When he nodded, her throat swelled more, cutting off her air. Growing light-headed, she shook her head. 'You knew all the time?'

'Only after you left this morning. I guessed there had to be more to the way you'd acted. I ended up discovering that you and I are more alike than you know.'

Her mind was caught in a whirlpool. She didn't know which way to turn or how to respond, especially to that last remark.

'Don't tell me you wear a prosthesis because that's something I wouldn't have missed.'

His smile was brief and...understanding. 'I know what it's like to live with the consequences of the past. To want to whitewash or, better yet, forget they ever happened.'

Her defences sprang up. 'I don't have anything to prove,' she lied.

'Then let me prove something to you.'

He kissed her again, this time with a deliberate care that asked for her consideration and her trust. When he angled down and swept her off her feet, this time she surrendered and didn't shy away. She did, however, think to murmur, 'Carrying me...you might hurt your shoulder.'

He began to walk. 'It'd be worth it.'

With her cradled in his arms, Alex crossed to the centre of the living room, then spotted a quilted bed beyond an opened door. Moving through, he manoeuvred to flick the light switch with his shoulder, but Libby stiffened.

'Could we leave the light off?'

Alex studied the concern in her gaze. Perhaps it was the bond they shared through love of their individual sports. Maybe it was as simple as sexual chemistry combining and setting off sparks that wouldn't die. Whatever the reason, in a short time Libby had come to mean far more than an early ticket back on the track or just another available female. What he'd learned about her accident made no difference to those feelings. But he needed to let her discover that in her own time. In her own way.

In the shadows he smiled into her eyes. 'Whatever you want.'

He crossed the room and, beside the bed, he set her on her feet, eased back the covers, then returned to trail a series of soft kisses around her jaw while he untied the gown's sash and carefully peeled the sleeves from her arms. The tip of his tongue drew a deliberate line from the tilt of her chin down the curve of her throat while his touch drifted and cupped to measure the sensual swell of her breasts. Groaning at the jolt of pleasure, he grazed the pads of his thumbs over her nipples, making the already tight beads harder still.

While her fingers combed his hair and she told him with a breathy sigh how wonderful he felt, he bit down against the urge to go about this consummation with a little more haste. If she thought he felt good, she felt better than heaven. Better than anyone, or anything, he'd known before.

He tugged the silk bow beneath her bust as his mouth worked soft scorching kisses along the sweep of her collarbone. When he slid the thin straps from her shoulders and her satin sheath fell to the floor, he lifted his head to hold her with his eyes while his erection throbbed and hardened more. In the dim light, he saw the wince, her gaze drop away, and all the breath left his lungs.

She'd never wanted him to know about her leg. Now she was worried over what he might say or think when she had nothing to hide behind. And for a terrifying heartbeat, he wasn't certain *what* to do. Libby was beautiful. More than anything, he wanted to make her feel that way. What if he somehow botched this by saying or doing something unintentionally thoughtless? Where his apprehensions over Annabelle were concerned, that had translated into saying and doing very little indeed. Damned if he'd turn away from this, but how should he reassure Libby?

But then a feeling—a unique sense of awareness—settled over him and, like a light turning green, he knew and could go forward. He only needed to be honest. In coming here tonight, he'd put himself out on a limb. Now he would do everything in his power to let her know it was safe to do the same. With every stroke, every kiss, he'd let her know he was glad their meeting had come to this. Most important, he hoped she felt the same way.

He cupped her shoulders and murmured close to her ear, 'I'm one very lucky man.'

He heard her intake of air at the same time she tipped slightly back. In the shadows, her wide luminous gaze met his, then, gradually, a guarded smile touched the corners of her mouth.

'I should warn you…it's been a while.'

He grazed his cheek tenderly against hers. 'Then we'd best make up for lost time.'

He swept her up and laid her on the sheet.

Libby was a quaking bundle of nerves. She wanted to do this, be with Alex this way, but she was also terrified to the marrow of her bones. One part of her cried out to trust him. He was a mature man who, better than many, understood about life; that she wore a prosthesis didn't factor into his feelings here. Another part, however, had reverted back to the uncertain, confused girl she'd been the first year after her accident. She felt lacking. Odd and incomplete.

But then he undressed, lay down, gathered her close and when his mouth covered hers again, those torturous dark feelings little by little fell away. Soon her arms went out, wrapping around his neck, then her fingers were splaying up through the back of his hair as they kissed hungrily, with all the passion they'd both tried at one time or another to deny.

Sighing into his mouth, she gave herself over to the magic. Let all her inhibitions wash away. The way he stroked her, adored her, was the highest form of bliss. Making love—*being* loved—had never felt like this.

When his lips left hers and his teeth grazed down one side of her throat, every nerve ending sizzled and her mind went to mush. Then he was dabbing warm firm kisses over her breasts, drawing one nipple into his mouth while he teased the other between a forefinger and thumb. All her other sensibilities fell away. She only knew his flesh on her flesh. Only felt his mounting desire stirring with hers. But when the caress of his mouth slid lower, and the glide of his hand did the same, all Libby's fears plumed up again, so thick and fast that they cut off her air.

On reflex, she gripped his hand.

In the misty light, his gaze snapped up and she saw his eyes round in surprise. He'd forgotten. Heck, she'd almost forgotten too.

Now, however, every muscle and tendon was gridlocked. Her heart was galloping but with an anticipation that had nothing to do with desire. In good faith, Alex might want to believe the state of her leg didn't matter, but, truth was, experience said that it did. And yet she hated herself for doubting his sincerity, for feeling this…diminished.

With a raw ache pressing on her chest and her stomach sinking fast, she closed her eyes, turned her head and gently but firmly urged his hand away.

Alex froze, as rigid and tense as Libby clearly was. He hadn't planned any moves. He was doing what felt good. What felt right. But as Libby had said, for her it had been a while. Had she not made love since her accident?

He wanted her to be comfortable with this. With him. At the same time, he wanted this joining to be everything it could be. Everything she deserved. For that to happen—to reassure her—he needed to persist. He wasn't giving up.

Tenderly, he brushed her cheek with the back of his hand. 'Did I hurt you?'

Keeping her eyes closed, facing away, she inhaled and shook her head. 'No.'

He tipped her chin toward him and waited until her glistening eyes dragged open. Then he willed her to feel, to understand. To find the kind of confidence in deep affection that could be borrowed from and fostered by another. That was here. She only needed to accept it.

In the soft shadows, he searched her eyes. 'Trust me, Libby. Trust yourself.'

Prepared to wait all night if need be, he smiled into her eyes and bit by bit the worry faded and her physical tension unlocked and eased. As he continued to stroke her cheek, gradually she began to smile too. When he was certain she was ready, when there was little chance she'd flinch again, he nuzzled against her neck and as his touch trailed lower—down her thigh, past that knee—he murmured near the shell of her ear.

'It makes no difference…it doesn't matter.…'

He gave her more time, letting his fingers glide, pressing meaningful kisses over her brow, at her temple. When her breathing had changed and he felt her stirring in that way that said she was drifting again, he let his mouth trail from her throat to the dip between her breasts. Finally his mouth closed over that pert tip again. As he drew her deeply in, her hips gradually arced up and his touch slid across.

He groaned with unreserved want.

She was so ready for him, wet and swollen.

He drew a flowing line up and down her cleft, then slowly circled and pressed that sensitive bud. When her hand wrapped around his and she trembled, he imagined her fire building, leaping higher, almost ready to consume. He could barely wait for the flames to take them both.

As her free palm fanned over and kneaded one shoulder, he moved up and stole another penetrating kiss while he brought her to the teetering brink. When she was trembling beneath him, he wove down the length of her body until he was kissing her again and hoping she could hold out longer even while feeling compelled to do everything within his power to make sure she couldn't.

Pleasure-filled noises hummed in her throat as he scooped under her behind and the tip of his tongue swirled and flicked. All too soon she was pressing down into the mattress, clutching the sheet, convulsing and flowing while her thighs clamped around his jaw.

He let her float all the way down before he slid back up and, in the shifting shadows, searched her eyes. They were happy, dreamy, more content than he had hoped. As her arms curved around the pillow beneath her head, with her hair splayed out, a silvery aura framing her glowing face, he knew he'd never know another moment like this, where he felt as if he'd seen and felt everything and yet still had so much to learn.

Libby slowly opened her eyes and put out her arms as the length of Alex's hard body joined with hers. Her mind was still spinning with tingling stars when he nudged inside. The pressure felt entirely natural and yet magical, like a king tide growing beneath a full moon, swelling so quickly, those stars were already building again. She arched up to meet him and, groaning against her lips, he thrust in deeply and all at once.

He hit a spot so high, so hot, she gripped his shoulders and gasped.

Pulling away, he combed the hair from her cheek and, concerned, searched her eyes. 'Libby, are you all right?'

Recovering, ready for more, she eased out a breath and nodded as her palms ran down his slick sides. 'Way better than all right.'

His smile came slowly. Then he filled her again. She felt his lidded eyes on her as the heat increased and the burn at her core condensed. When she didn't think the friction he'd built could spark any brighter, his movements came faster, he drove in harder and a moan escaped her throat. She'd given herself over totally to this delicious sizzling sensation…the intense force boiling through her blood.

When the pressure seemed too much, when she was on the scorching cusp again—

He dropped his head into her hair and, inhaling the floral scent, let the tide rise to an unprecedented high. He murmured her name, drove in to the hilt and held himself there, deep inside, while she moved and clutched around him. He didn't want the feeling to end, never wanted to let her go. The force was so great. The pleasure too extreme.

At the instant his orgasm imploded, Alex arced his neck back and gave into the shuddering release that rocked every cell in his body. The climax throbbed again and again, and all the while a chorus hummed through his head and his heart.

I'm one very lucky man...

Gazing through her bedroom window, Libby watched the glittering stars, listened to the rolling surf and cuddled up against her scrumptious man. After making love again she felt both exhausted and raised up. Her every surface buzzed from his attentions. Her mouth and breasts burned from the graze of his stubble. She'd never been more sated. Never wanted to know anything again so much.

Alex Wolfe was more than she could ever have imagined.

His deep voice rumbled out from the shadows. 'You sleepy?'

'No.' She snuggled in closer. 'You?'

Rolling to face her, he drew a tender line around her cheek. 'Wide awake.'

Libby blew out a quiet contented breath. Was it imagination or did he feel as blissful lying here as she did? Amazing, given she'd had little to no confidence these past few years as far as intimacy with a man was concerned. This was the first time she'd made love since before her accident but, with his help, she'd overcome her nerves. In fact, she felt more whole and desirable than she ever had.

For long peaceful moments, she lay there, absorbing the way he watched his fingers toy with her hair, sweeping back strands, curling a section behind her ear.

'I bet you looked unbelievable on a board,' he said.

She held her breath but the regret she sometimes felt when she recalled that lost part of her life didn't surface. Rather, this time when she thought back, she was filled with nothing but a sense of happy nostalgia.

'It came naturally,' she said. 'My gran said I could swim before I could walk.'

'Guess our talents come out early. I rode a push-bike at a little over two. Was doing stunts and mad stuff when I was six.' He touched his nose. 'Almost lost this when I came off shooting down a hill at warp speed.'

Imagining the blood, she flinched. 'Your mother must've been beside herself.'

A muscle in his jaw flexed. 'My mother died before my second birthday. Drug overdose.'

Libby's heart sunk. She couldn't imagine it. She'd known his childhood had been tough but to have lost a mother as well, and in such circumstances…'You wouldn't remember anything about her, then.'

From the wooden look on his face, she thought he might simply close the subject. He often looked so troubled when talk turned to his past. But then he tugged his ear and even found a lopsided smile.

'Apparently Amber, my mother, was a bit of a party girl but not much good at bath times or changing nappies. Still, from what I was told she loved her children. There are snaps of her dressing us up for games, taking us to the beach to build massive sandcastles. William even came along a couple of times. In their own unhealthy way, I think my parents might have been happy. Amber seemed to bring out the best, as well as the worst, in him. A lot of people did.'

He dropped his gaze but not before she glimpsed the pain and regret lurking in the shadows of his eyes. Clearly he hadn't meant to go that deeply into it. Given just how dark his past was, she more than respected that. She wished she could go back in time and protect the innocent little boy Alex once had been. Since she couldn't, perhaps shedding a bit more light on her own yesterdays might help.

'I was surfing up in North Queensland on holiday with a friend when my accident happened,' she began. 'It was my fault. I should have been more careful.'

Focused again, he pushed up on one elbow. 'In what way?'

'Firstly, I should've waited for my friend before I plunged in. There was nobody else around. Number one rule broken.'

'If you get in trouble there's no one to help.'

She nodded. 'An onshore breeze was forecast. They turn a good swell to mush. But that morning when I first ran in, the waves were pumping.'

A shiver chased over her skin and she shrugged. 'I didn't realise there was coral nearby. After twenty minutes or so, I did see the fin, however. That's when I decided to double time it back in.'

He held her hand and squeezed. 'A shark.'

'I found out later it'd been cruising the bay for weeks. Should have done my homework. I caught a last wave in but it closed down.' She explained, 'The wave broke along its entire length all at once. When I wiped out, I felt a stab on my calf—the coral—and came up disorientated. I'm grateful I didn't see the fin a second time. Just felt the tug.'

His face pinched, Alex swore under his breath and squeezed her hand again.

'My buddy had arrived in time to see my spill.' She smiled, remembering how brave Barb had been. 'I've never been able to thank her enough for swimming out and saving me. She did what she could using regular first aid know-how, but we were miles from civilisation, surrounded by sand and palm trees. She sent out an SOS on her phone. A rescue boat patrolling close by picked us up. At first the doctors thought they could save my lower limb but an infection set in and, well... that was that.'

He blew out a long breath. 'My shoulder injury seems pathetic compared to what you've gone through.'

'It was hard at first.' She thought more. 'Confusing, really. But I was walking six months later. These days, people who don't know about the accident can't tell.'

'How do you feel when you go into the water now?'

She tugged the blanket up around her neck. 'I haven't been in since.'

'There must be a part of you that wants to?'

Her stomach muscles knotted. Odd. She could recall that day, her injury and recuperation, and be as close to okay with it as a person could be. But the thought of going back in the water...

Shuddering, she drew the blanket higher still.

She didn't want to push herself that far. She simply wouldn't feel safe. But fearless Alex Wolfe didn't need to know that. Tonight she didn't want a pity party, then a pep talk.

'One day I might,' she said lightly, then added more truthfully, 'I bought an apartment on the esplanade so I'd be close to the sound and smell of the ocean. Hasn't enticed me yet.'

He lifted her hand and pressed his lips to her inside wrist. 'You must have had good people there for you afterward.'

'Unfortunately one of them wasn't my boyfriend.' When Alex's brows jumped, she qualified, 'Fiancé actually. We'd planned to be married.'

A growl rumbled in his throat. 'Please don't tell me he dumped you because of the accident.'

'Scott was a surfing pro with titles like me. We both lived for the water. At the time it seemed we lived for each other. We surfed the world's hot spots together. We were both totally dedicated to our sport. But after my accident, things changed. *I* changed. Scott didn't have too deep of an insight into how my injury had affected me…affected every aspect of my life. Truth was he wasn't much interested in spending the time or the effort to try to understand. Seemed if we couldn't surf together,' she explained, 'we had absolutely nothing in common.'

She cast her mind back and felt that same twinge of regret and awareness she'd acknowledged back then.

'Scott came to see me less and less often,' she went on. 'When he did visit, we had little to say. Our relationship had been that superficial—more about how I looked hanging off his arm at events than anything.'

She didn't add that he'd never touched her again after her injury, although from Alex's keen expression she wondered if he'd guessed.

Alex's voice resonated in the semi-darkness. 'So he broke it off.'

'I did. When I realised how separate we felt without the ocean bringing us together, seemed there was only one choice.'

Alex grunted. 'I hope he and his surfboard are happy together.'

She gave a wry grin. 'I'm sure they are. And I'm not bitter about that. I had friends who were fabulous through the whole thing. My parents, and Gran, of course…even when I was being a pain and down on myself,' she admitted.

When he brought her close and grazed his lips over her crown, she closed her eyes and absorbed his masculine smell as well as his strength.

'You're being too hard on yourself,' he murmured.

She didn't bother saying she knew that she

wasn't. But she'd survived—and flourished, in some ways, at least. Tonight with Alex had helped even more.

'I needed something else I could put my heart and soul into,' she said. 'Turned out to be something that I ended up believing in a thousand times more than collecting sports awards.'

'Helping others recover from their injuries. And you're wonderful at it.'

Her heart swelled. 'You really think so?'

'I know I've given you a rough time but I appreciate everything you've done. In fact, I think I'm in need of a little therapy right now.'

Alarmed, she studied his eyes for signs of physical pain. They had been pretty energetic beneath the sheets. 'Is your shoulder hurting?'

'Higher. A little ache—' he tapped his lips '—right here.'

Relaxing, she laughed. 'I can fix that.' She came forward and her kiss skimmed his bristled jaw. 'How does that feel? Or maybe I should try this technique.' Her tongue slid down to the beating hollow at the base of his throat.

He rolled her over and murmured against her parted lips, 'Libby, I'm aching all over.'

CHAPTER NINE

THAT morning he and Libby ate breakfast at a local Manly café.

With the waves washing on the beach and traffic, both pedestrian and motor, passing at a leisurely weekend clip, they took an outside table and enjoyed the perfect autumn sunshine while ordering—fruit and toast for the lady, a full breakfast with bacon, eggs, fried mushrooms and tomatoes for him. He'd worked up quite an appetite, Alex realised, setting his napkin on his lap and considering something sweet to finish with…not that he hadn't enjoyed 'sweet' all night long.

There had been a sour note, however, when Libby had told him about her so-called fiancé. She had to know she was better off without that dolt. What kind of a man would commit himself by giving a beautiful girl a ring and then—

The fork stopped midway to Alex's mouth.

What had happened to Libby's engagement ring?

Was that why she wasn't into jewellery now? Bad memories of a lying solitaire?

Alex stabbed more egg on his fork.

He hoped she'd dropped it in an express post bag and sent it back to that son of a—

'Do you eat like that every morning?'

Snapping back, Alex assembled a smile. 'Today I was famished.' Before he brought the fork to his mouth again, he added, 'That's your fault.'

'We didn't get much sleep,' she admitted beneath lowered lashes as he chewed and set his cutlery aside.

'Sleep's overrated.'

'Why sleep when you can race, right?' She slanted her head and a waterfall of silvery blond cascaded over her shoulder as she leaned back. 'How did it all start? You mentioned taking your father's cars out and earning yourself a reputation.'

Needing time, Alex patted his mouth with the napkin. The subject of his father could get tricky. Plainly put, he didn't like to discuss it. The topic caused his insides to crawl and made him ashamed that his last name was Wolfe. Still, if Libby had the courage to open up and come clean about her slug of an ex…

Alex cleared his throat and sat back.

Guess he could share a little more.

'The first time I took off,' he began, 'I wasn't quite fourteen. My father…' Alex's throat tightened and he grunted, remembering too well. 'William was being his usual obnoxious self. I needed to escape so I lifted his favourite sports car and tore off. That's the moment I knew what I wanted to do. How I wanted to live. I felt at home with the top down, the wind on my face, racing away as fast as four wheels could take me.'

Like it was yesterday, he recalled the thrill of that first time pitting himself against the curves and dips in the road, against the bona fide danger of excess speed. It never got old.

'And your father never caught you?'

Before he could contain it, Alex flinched. In time he hid the subsequent shudder. No wonder he'd rather not speak of those days. Preferred never to think of them, full stop.

Reaching for his juice, he resumed his more casual mask. 'Eventually he caught me. By that time, sneaking out with one of his cars had got to be addictive…a regular event. He used to spot a scratch or dent now and then.'

The beatings that followed had been worth every minute he'd got to spend behind the wheel.

Libby's glistening eyes said she didn't know whether to be amused or shocked. 'You're lucky you didn't kill yourself. Or someone else.'

Of course she was right. Thank God he'd hooked up with someone who had taught him early about respect—for himself, for cars, as well for others on the road.

'If it's any compensation, my joyrides got me expelled at the end of summer term '91.'

Her face fell. 'Oh, Alex…'

'They also got me noticed by a gang who loved fast cars as much as I did.' He smiled. Good times. 'I bought myself a souped-up dirt bike and competed with the other guys in weekend meets. That's where I got a taste for winning. We had our own races organised in the back streets on quiet weekends.'

Her smile was wry. 'Sounds like a wild crowd.'

'There were some parties,' he admitted, taking a sip of his drink. Given that last one… He set down his glass and pinned back his shoulders. 'Probably too many parties.'

But that was a whole other story and one he refused to broach with Libby now. With anyone *any time*.

A touch on his arm had him glancing up to find her worried gaze.

'Alex…you okay?'

He shook off the image of Annabelle after that night and pasted on a smile. 'Fine. I'm fine.'

'Did you ever get in trouble with the law?' she asked.

'There was one night,' he said carefully. 'A

policeman took pity on me. Said he'd look the other way if I put my so-called talent to good use rather than playing the lunatic. He gave me the name of a racing buddy of his. A mechanic in Oxfordshire.'

Elbow on the table, she set her cheek in the bed of her hand. 'And he took you under his wing?'

That's when life took its first good turn.

'Carter White became my coach in life as well as on the track.' Alex's chest grew warm the way it did whenever he thought of the difference that one man had made. 'When I first went to his shop, I wanted to jump in the first car I could and tear up the road. But Carter taught me to value my skill and the vehicles I drove. He also made me promise to catch up on classes I'd missed after I was expelled for truancy.'

'I thought you said you were expelled because of joyriding.'

His grin was lopsided. 'That too.'

She coughed out a laugh. 'Did this Carter White own a bag of fairy dust? How did he manage to turn such a wayward kid around?'

'With a chronically slow and steady approach.' Much like the technique Libby used on his shoulder, come to think of it. 'He had me work on cars and motorbikes for months before he let me drive or ride. At first I thought he was doing it simply to annoy me, but it didn't take long before I learned a deep appreciation for the way engines worked, the way bodies were put together. I learned to admire their beauty and power. After five years as a team, I thanked him and took off to pursue the bright lights.'

'Just like that?'

Her brows knitted…as if she thought he ought to have stayed?

'It was with his blessing,' Alex pointed out. Carter had wanted his protégé to advance as much as Alex had needed to move on. 'He gave me a memento of our time together and to remember the faith he'd put in me. He made the medal himself. It has a big number one plunging through its centre.' Anyone who cared to read up on Alex Wolfe knew about the significance of that piece. 'Whenever and wherever I race, I carry that medal for good luck'. Ironic that after Annabelle's last message he'd forgotten to slip it into his suit before his crash. He'd never forget it again.

'It means a great deal to you.'

Understatement. 'That chunk of metal means more than all the cups and trophies I could acquire in a lifetime of championships.'

It represented not only everything he'd gained but everything he'd left behind and never wanted to visit again. Carter had told him to pass it on when he didn't need it anymore. To give it to someone who did. Hell, he'd rather cut out his own heart.

He could never give it up, just as he could never give up racing.

'When did you see him last?' she asked.

And Alex's breath caught in his chest. He couldn't remember the last time. He glossed over it.

'We keep in touch.'

'By email?'

He thought about it and nodded. 'Usually.'

Her gaze probed his as if she wanted to dig more but then she carried on with her earlier thread.

'They say you're fearless on the track. That there's never been a more focused champion.'

With a jaded grin, he gestured for the bill. 'Guess the press are good for something.'

'Did the other Wolfe children go off the rails before making good?'

God knows they'd all had their moments. 'The second eldest, Lucas, was always a handful. He never knew his mother. Never even knew her name. He was dropped on the Wolfe Manor doorstep when he was a newborn.' He squashed a spike of unease. Poor bastard. 'Our father took a particular dislike to him. Can't blame Luc for growing up to like women and booze a bit too much. But in her most recent email Annabelle said our shameless playboy sibling has found true love.' His grin was warm. 'Difficult to believe. She must be an exceptional girl.'

Alex's thoughts again turned to the woman sitting across from him. Seemed he'd met an exceptional woman too. Not that he was after marriage. Time, lifestyle, an unhappy childhood without parents…there were a hundred reasons to remain single. Where women were concerned, he was careful not to insinuate anything else. He had never and *would* never promise what he couldn't deliver. Not like the jerk who'd let Libby down.

'What about Jacob?' she asked. 'Didn't you wonder about him after he walked out and never came back?'

'He…had a lot weighing on his mind.'

She cocked her head as if trying to read his expression. 'Sounds as if you all had terrible things to reconcile.'

'Jacob perhaps more than any of us.'

Alex's back teeth ground together. He'd like to be completely honest but he didn't discuss that particular episode of his life. Still, sitting here with Libby now…

For the first time in his life Alex felt an urge to open up.

'A year before Jacob left there was…an incident,' he said. 'Charges were laid.'

Her face paled. 'Serious charges?'

The waiter left the bill. Alex scrawled his signature and set the pen down. 'Want to walk for a while?'

She scraped back her chair. 'Love to.'

Five minutes later, they were strolling along the esplanade, the road on one side and the tumbling surf on the other. He wound his arm around her waist, then, looking out over the glittering blue-green waves, asked, 'You okay with this?' *Being so close to the water?*

With the breeze combing through her flaxen hair, she nodded. 'I often walk along here. Just haven't managed to get any sand between my toes lately.' She snuggled up against his arm. 'But we were talking about Jacob.'

Alex focused and suddenly all those old fettered memories strained to break free, pinpricks of murky light struggling through tears in a dark smelly rag. Looking back he didn't know how he'd ever lived through those tragic years. How any of the Wolfe children had. But that was the secret, he supposed. Even with storms of brutality and madness and death swirling all around, the Wolfe kids had remained individual and strong—he grinned to himself—like bamboo.

'My father had a foul temper,' he began, looking out over today's thunderous waves crashing on the shore, 'which was a hundred times worse when he drank. And he drank often. We all suffered at his hand. All but one. Then one night—'

He bit off the rest. He didn't need to go there.

Libby jumped to her own conclusion. 'Alex, your father didn't *kill* anyone?'

'He might as well have.'

'Who?'

Alex's gut wrenched. Even now those memories left him stone-cold. He blew out a long steadying breath and grated out the words he'd never wanted to utter.

'He assaulted my sister.'

Libby's heels dug into the pavement as her face filled first with anger, then with pain.

'Annabelle?'

'He'd been out riding all day. Drinking most of it too. When Annabelle came home he said she wasn't dressed appropriately.'

Alex remembered the micro mini, skyscraper heels and carefully applied makeup Annabelle had worn that night. She hadn't looked like a fourteen-year-old. She'd looked more like a woman who knew precisely what was what. Truth was that Annabelle *was* an innocent. Or had been until that evening when innocence had been destroyed forever.

'Our father railed at her, then pulled out his riding crop....'

Closing his eyes, Alex tried to shut out the scene he'd heard about second-hand. He couldn't bring himself to say the words. To face the shame. His father's or his own.

Libby had covered her mouth but her gasp escaped. 'That poor girl.'

Alex studied her face. Libby had no idea that the revulsion she felt was as much his to bear as his father's. Of all his siblings, he loved Annabelle best and yet he'd let her down, fobbed her off, when he should have been there to look out for her. Thank God Jacob came home when he did.

'Jacob tried to protect her and pushed William away,' he went on, his pace down to a crawl now. 'My father staggered back and struck his head on the corner of the staircase. He died instantly.'

'But surely it was self-defence.'

'The jury acquitted my brother of all charges. But the weight of what he'd done ate away at Jacob.'

It sure as hell had eaten away at *him*.

Her gaze filled with sympathy and support, Libby stopped and held his gaze. 'Do you and Annabelle ever talk about it?'

His stomach lurched and he frowned. The very idea knocked him completely off balance.

'Why *would* we?'

He'd all but snapped it out, and Libby blinked several times before her gaze sharpened, trying to see through to places he didn't care for her to go.

'Is there something more, Alex?' she asked quietly. 'Something you're not telling me?'

His heartbeat thumping, he started off again.

He'd said enough. The incident had forever changed his sister and it was largely his fault. How could he and Annabelle ever talk about such cruelty, about her maiming—

'Alex…?'

He brought himself back and was about to change the subject when a group, congregated around a picnic table, caught his attention. One woman held a folded magazine and was pointing their way. Looked like he was back in the news.

Defiant, he lifted his chin.

And so what if he was? His arm was out of its sling. Thanks to Libby, he was on his way to full recovery and after two and some weeks cooped up, worried about his future, he felt the greatest urge to venture out.

His gaze slid to his companion. Maybe she'd enjoy a break as well, to continue what they'd started here. Something fun and light, of course. Like the past few hours had been.

As the thought took form, his mouth went dry and Alex wanted to laugh. He was *nervous* about inviting Libby? Amazing what a couple of weeks away from regular social contact could do. She wouldn't say no.

Would she?

He cleared his throat, tugged his ear. 'What would you say to getting out of here for a while?'

She tossed a wary look around. 'You mean, off the street?'

'I mean out of Sydney.'

Libby froze. She'd heard Alex's suggestion. That he—that *they*—should escape the city. And when the shock wore off, her first reaction was to clasp her hands and exclaim, 'When do we head out?' What girl, who'd spent the night with such an amazing man, would think to refuse?

But at the same time a cloud blocked out the sun, darker reality sank in.

She glanced around. Alex's presence radiated out even in this casual crowd, same way his charisma had turned heads in that Malaysian restaurant. An animated group by that picnic table had certainly picked up on who he was. It seemed, now that his shoulder was on its way to full recovery, he was no longer reticent about getting out and being seen. He didn't seem perturbed by that crowd's attention. Wherever he went, he'd be noticed. Which meant, if she were with him, she'd be noticed too.

Two things wrong with that.

Firstly, she didn't think it wise to make a habit of parading around with Alex as if they were romantically involved, which, she guessed, they were. Even here, in relatively relaxed Manly, people had phones with cameras and video capabilities and weren't afraid to use them. Maybe Alex accepted those kinds of intrusions into his private world but she was no longer a celebrity and didn't miss the spotlight. She didn't need her life, present or past, speculated upon in magazines or the internet.

He wanted to whisk her away?

While her teeth rolled over her bottom lip, he raised a brow.

'I see you're not racing home to pack a bag.'

'Alex, what if you're recognised?' She rephrased. 'Make that, what happens *when* you're recognised?'

'And someone snaps our picture for some celebrity magazine?' He leaned forward and stage whispered. 'We'll survive.'

He'd survive. But, 'You can understand that the perception that I'm involved with a high-profile client could damage my career.'

'We could wear dark glasses and Hungarian moustaches?'

He chuckled and, despite it all, she smiled too. Was she overreacting? Like she had when she'd thought he wouldn't be interested if he found out about her leg?

'Look,' he said more levelly, 'if you'd rather not, we'll stay in. I understand you want to shield yourself.'

She sighed. Now she felt bad.

What was so wrong with being the girl who'd experienced an incredible night and couldn't deny herself more? Life could be uncertain, but there didn't have to be a shark lurking behind every shadow. She'd felt so safe with Alex these past few hours. Where was the crime in wanting to prolong that?

She made a decision. Stood up tall.

'No. I want to go.'

He gauged her expression. 'You're certain?'

Libby held her breath. Her head told her not to go but her heart was saying loud and clear, *What's the worst that can happen?*

The sun came out at the same time she smiled broadly and announced, 'Commander, lead the way.'

Eli was sitting on the forecourt steps when Alex arrived home an hour later. Alex bet the magazine his assistant held was the same edition the picnic table crowd had been ogling earlier. Obviously it contained a shot of him. A file shot speculating on his comeback? Or had he somehow been snapped in Sydney these past weeks?

As Alex swung out of the limo and the driver headed off, Eli pushed to his feet. Alex's step slowed on his way up the steps. His friend's expression was closed. Not a good sign.

Eli offered the magazine, folded to a celebrity page. 'No prizes for guessing where you spent the night.'

Alex zoomed in on a picture; a chill sped up his spine and he swore.

Eli scratched his temple. 'I, er, take it you weren't aware this was out?'

'I…had some idea.'

Alex let them inside and headed toward the office, that photograph imprinted at the forefront of his mind—he and Libby standing outside her apartment building, embracing. Kissing.

'Her face is hidden,' Eli said, following Alex down the hall. 'And her name isn't listed, but people will want to know who your new love interest is. What'll I say when the phone starts ringing?'

'No comment.'

'They'll find out one way or another. Could be better coming from us.'

Alex swept into his office, fell into the chair behind his desk and came clean.

'I asked Libby to come away with me this weekend.'

Eli's brows jumped, then he slid his hands into his trouser pockets. 'Somewhere secluded?'

'I was thinking the Gold Coast.'

When Libby had brought up her concerns over how she might be perceived should the press spot them together, he'd acquiesced. Speculations about sleeping with a high-profile client…He understood Libby wanted to look out for her reputation. But he was pleased she'd decided to go with her heart and had agreed to a quick trip away. After this, however…

Eli sauntered forward. 'I might be wrong but when I spoke with Libby Henderson she didn't seem the type to want back in the limelight. In fact, she seemed reserved. Private.'

'Anyone knows if you work with celebrities some of the shine is bound to rub off.'

'She's doing more than *working* with you.'

Alex's gaze snapped up from his hands, clasped on the desk. 'She's over twenty-one.'

Eli's nostrils flared, then he held up his hands. 'You're right. It's none of my business.'

Alex scooted the chair over to his laptop.

Eli was dead on. It wasn't his business.

After tapping a few keys, images of a cosmopolitan skyline, bordered by miles of golden beach, flashed onto the screen. An hour's flight, relaxed and at the same time full of life. Just the place for an overnight escape.

'Can you organise the jet to fly out for the Gold Coast this afternoon at three?' Alex asked his assistant. 'I'll need a car and driver at the airport and reservations for a penthouse suite at the casino.'

'Nothing like keeping a low profile,' Eli muttered.

Alex ignored it. 'Book tickets for the show too.'

'And if it's booked out?'

Alex pasted on a smile. 'As always, I know you'll come through.'

When Eli saluted his chief and strode out to get plans underway, Alex sat back and took stock.

He shouldn't be cut at Eli for having his say. That's what he paid him for and he only had his and Libby's best interests at heart. Certainly Libby was a nice lady who ought to be treated well—protected—particularly after that failed episode with her ex. But, as he'd told Eli, he wasn't taking advantage of Libby. She was an adult who wanted to make the most of what they'd shared while they could. She wouldn't be thinking long-term, not when she knew better than most how his work ate up practically all his time and energy.

Simply put, he wasn't the marrying kind. Eli knew it. All the *world* knew it. After hearing more of his lacklustre childhood today, surely Libby was smart enough to know it too.

CHAPTER TEN

As COMMERCIAL as the Gold Coast had become, Libby had always adored this laidback yet glitzy part of the world. Many considered the beaches to be the whitest and finest of any. The restaurants and nightlife were first-rate. Still, when Alex had invited her to join him on a one-night whirlwind stay at Jupiters Casino at Broadbeach, initially she'd been reluctant. Even landing at Coolangatta Airport fifteen minutes earlier, despite her enthusiasm in accepting, she'd still had her doubts.

Catching a sidelong glance at Alex's classic profile now, sitting alongside him in another chauffeur-driven limo, Libby's cheeks toasted remembering the glorious hours they'd spent together last night. This morning when they'd woken and had gone to breakfast, she'd felt so comfortable in his company, almost as if they'd been 'a couple' for years. Alex had delved more into his childhood and the shocking Wolfe family secrets. She'd ended up all the more in awe of what this man had achieved under such oppressive conditions growing up. She also felt lucky to know that he trusted her enough to share the information. She trusted him more now too. Coming away with Alex this weekend felt right. If a photographer happened to catch them together…

Her hands locking in her lap, she focused out the limo window at the beach shacks intermingled with high-rise resorts flying by.

She needed to take one step at a time…even if secretly she'd caught herself daydreaming about joining Alex on other flights, to Spain, Turkey, Monte Carlo… She shouldn't let her imagination roam like that, but they seemed well suited on so many levels, not least of all in the bedroom. When they were together, she didn't think about her deficiencies. She only felt desired and beautiful.

Of course she wasn't anywhere near as refined as the women he usually dated. Not anywhere near as glamorous. But the way Alex had treated and confided in her, she was convinced he wasn't as shallow and mercenary as she'd first thought. In fact, he was anything but.

Alex's voice broke into her thoughts.

'I did mention the show tonight.'

Knowing the production, Libby crooned out a line about still calling Australia home and, while Alex chuckled, she added, 'I've heard it's fabulous.'

'You like music?'

'Sure.'

'Dancing?'

'Oh, I haven't danced in years.'

'We'll have to change that.'

In all honestly she wouldn't say that she *couldn't* dance. Despite her prosthesis she was certain she had the stability and balance needed. Handling the surf was a different matter. In the ocean your balance was constantly challenged. When she'd been younger, leaping over the waves had seemed as natural and fun as eating ice cream. Now she could barely bring herself to think about finding the courage to venture out again.

The limo eased up the casino's resort-style drive. The massive tiered building had been visible from the road for some time. With the huge orange sun sinking rapidly behind the hinterland horizon, banks of lights began to flicker on—iridescent gold and blue—creating the image of a colossal elaborate staircase, which led to the complex's middle floors. The grounds were pristine and subtropical with masses of palm trees and colourful seasonal flowers in bloom. Libby felt as if she'd truly arrived in paradise.

As the limo rolled into the forecourt, a uniformed doorman strode up and opened the passenger's door. Alex assisted her out and together they entered an establishment where multiple millions were gambled, won and lost, each day. Moving into the lobby, Alex kept his sunglasses on, surely not because he thought they might disguise who he was. He couldn't walk into a room and go unnoticed anymore than Russell Crowe. From the way her green eyes widened, the brunette behind the reception desk knew precisely who this handsome guest was.

After checking in, they rode a lift to the top, while peering down over the lower floors through the clear windows of the cabin. When he opened the door of their penthouse and ushered her inside, overwhelmed, Libby sighed long and loud. She felt thoroughly spoilt by the plush crimson carpet, extravagant matching window dressings and sumptuous leather furnishings. But she also felt strangely at home, or at least more at home than in Alex's grand Rose Bay residence. His house was beyond beautiful, but so large and a little sterile for her tastes. This suite, on the other hand, was big but also had colour and something of a cosy feel even amid all the crystal and gold fittings. She just knew they'd have a wonderful time here.

Alex wandered up behind her. His arms slid around her waist as his warm lips nuzzled her ear.

'You like?'

Smiling, she nodded. 'It's gorgeous.'

'I could extend our reservation.'

Her heart leapt, but there was no way. 'I have to be back in the office Monday.'

His hands skimmed down the front of her trousers. 'No chance of putting back your appointments?'

She didn't bother to reply. He knew her well enough to understand she would never put her personal agenda ahead of clients' prearranged appointments.

He chuckled against the sensitive sweep of her neck. 'I'll take that as a no. So until Sunday night, then—' he eased her around '—let's focus on us.'

He tilted her chin up, his mouth covered hers and the effects of his kiss spiralled through her centre, leaving her weak and instantly wanting. She'd been right agreeing to come here with Alex today. Everything felt so perfect. His body pressed against hers. His words. Most of all, his kiss.

His lips left hers slowly but his mouth stayed close. 'You sure you want to go see this show? We could always stay in.'

Libby's pulse rate leapt. She was tempted but, 'I'm sure the tickets weren't easy to get a hold of.'

'Neither were you.' He took her handbag and blindly set it on the lounge while his eyes smouldered into hers. 'I'll order up champagne and we can sip it in bed.'

In the middle of another penetrating kiss, Alex's phone buzzed and he mumbled, 'Ignore it.'

Dreamy, she murmured back, 'Could be important.'

'Don't care.'

When the buzz sounded again, however, he groaned and reached for his phone. About to turn it off, he looked at the message ID and drew in a quick breath.

'It's Annabelle.'

He retrieved the message. When his brows crept in, Libby asked, 'Is something wrong?'

'She's texting to see if I'll be attending Nathaniel's wedding next weekend. I've already said I'll be racing.'

Libby's insides pitched. He meant racing at his all-important Round Four in China. Holding her stomach, she moved off toward the palm-and-surf-fringed view. She couldn't avoid it any longer.

'We're actually not certain about that yet.'

Feeling his eyes boring a hole in her back, Libby waited on tenterhooks. Although from the get-go she'd known that he'd planned to have her sign off on his injury before the stipulated six weeks, she'd never agreed to anything. Neither had she dismissed his goal outright. Nothing was impossible. Similarly nothing was set in cement.

In the preceding weeks, she'd wrangled her way

around the issue. Now, for more reasons than one, she needed to be clear.

Assuming her professional mask, she rotated around. 'Your shoulder is doing extremely well. But given that your doctor was firm about the time frame for recovery, I can't make any decisions for or against just yet.'

His eyes narrowed. She could sense his mind ticking over as his chin came slowly up and he sauntered toward her. 'You could give me a full evaluation early.'

'Your cuff and lesser muscles have been under a great deal of strain, and after the setback yesterday—'

'There's no reason we can't go through the exercise, is there?'

Well…

Cornered, she exhaled. 'No. There's no reason.'

'Then I'd like the evaluation.' The tension in his jaw eased but his gaze still held that glint.

'I need you to know that I won't falsify my records.' She wouldn't do that for anyone for any reason. He must know that.

His gaze probed hers and a slight grin hooked one corner of his mouth. 'Of course you wouldn't.'

As her heartbeat thudded, she tried to read his eyes.

When they'd first met she'd believed she'd had

his number. Nothing was taboo when it came to Alex Wolfe securing what he needed to benefit his racing career, including seducing his physiotherapist. Remarkably, in the past twenty-four hours, she'd come to respect Alex. Last night, this morning, flying here this afternoon, she'd even come to trust him…trust that he wouldn't intentionally use or hurt her. Whatever his plans before they'd met, he would never try to manipulate her now.

'When do you need to let your doctor know?' she asked.

'I can call him Monday with a standby and give the heads-up as late as Wednesday.'

She kept her gaze on his, then eyed his injured shoulder, which looked as magnificent as the other beneath his casual cream button-down *sans* tie. He'd been superbly fit to begin with. His muscles and tendons had responded well to her program. In her opinion he wasn't there yet…

But if they had until Wednesday and she tested his shoulder then, holding absolutely nothing back…

She tilted her head. She had to ask.

'And if I decide your shoulder's not fit to race?'

He shrugged. 'Then we'll go to my brother's wedding in London.'

She coughed out a laugh, then realised he was

serious. 'You said your other brother's hotel is off the coast of *South America.*'

'Yes, but Sebastian owns hotels worldwide. He has another hotel in London, that's where the wedding is being held. You have a passport?'

The room began to spin. Alex was asking her to a wedding? And not just *any* wedding. A Wolfe family occasion, with his brothers and the twin sister he so clearly adored. And missed, though he didn't want to admit it.

'I'd much rather take you to China with me,' he added, closing the distance left separating them. 'But let's make the Grande Wolfe Hotel our backup plan. For now...' He took her hand and led her to the bedroom. 'Let's not wait for champagne.'

They dined in an award-winning restaurant overlooking the casino's dazzling atrium. The redwood and granite decor was exquisite, a perfect setting for the haute cuisine. They enjoyed basil salmon terrine and roast duckling before moving into the theatre to view a show that equalled in talent and score any lavish Vegas production.

Afterward, when they crossed out into the main area, close to where the gaming took place, Libby had thought she, at least, should be tired; the previous night had been a long one and she was an early-to-bed type of girl. And yet this evening had been so enlivening, the atmosphere so electric, she couldn't think about retiring to the quiet of their suite just yet. It was as if her every cell was on celebratory mode. Particularly when she thought about his suggestion that she accompany him to the Wolfe wedding. She would get to meet all the larger-than-life characters she'd heard so much about.

It all seemed surreal.

Of course, she couldn't pretend that she was the kind of woman others might expect to see accompanying Alex to such an event. She didn't have a manicure every week, or worry too much about fashion and A-lists. Eventually, she supposed, word would leak that she and Alex were involved. And when it did, what anyone else thought wouldn't matter.

But she was thinking too far ahead.

Slipping through the crowd, looking like the silver screen's latest version of James Bond in his dinner suit, Alex wrapped her arm around his and slid over a wicked grin.

'I think you ought to wear that gown to therapy Monday morning, doc.'

Libby swallowed a laugh. She did feel a little like a princess in this evening dress, which she'd bought for the physio guest speaker dinner next month. Beneath the sweetheart neckline, the strapless bodice, which was decorated with beads, fit snug to the hips. The gold leaf coloured satin skirt fell straight to the floor and featured an elegant chapel train. Beyond beautiful to wear on a special evening, however…

She arched a brow. 'It wouldn't be so practical in your gym.'

'Who cares about practical?' He came close, nipped her ear and a bevy of tingles flew through her. 'Will we put a few in the slot machines?' he asked, changing the subject as he tipped away. 'Or are you more a blackjack fan?'

'I know we're in a casino, but I don't gamble. I don't mind watching the excitement though.'

He studied a croupier sweeping a tower of chips to the house and admitted, 'Not my vice either.' His eyes flashed. 'I know what I promised we'd do. *Dance.*'

Libby stilled. She was so not comfortable with that idea, but she didn't want to seem like a coward. Or…inadequate.

Casting a quick glance around at patrons enjoying the beating lights and ringing bells, she hitched up her shoulders and let them drop. 'I don't think they have a dance floor.'

'Of course they do.' His eyes lighting up, he snapped his fingers. 'I have an idea.'

Before she could object, they were headed toward the reception desk. After leaving her by an elaborate water feature, he stopped by the concierge and spoke briefly to a middle-aged man who nodded enthusiastically and handed something over. Joining her again, Alex snatched a kiss from her cheek.

'All set.'

He wouldn't explain further, only led her to the casino foyer and out into the forecourt, where a sleek black sports car awaited. When a uniformed porter opened the passenger's side door, Libby hesitated only a moment before giving into the spirit of adventure and sliding into the sumptuous dark leather cabin. After buckling up, Alex ignited the engine and, incredibly low to the ground, the car zipped out the hotel grounds.

Anticipation balling in her stomach, Libby looked across and took in Alex's classic profile, dramatically silhouetted against the moon and streetlights. 'So, where are you whisking me away to now?'

His mouth hooked into a grin. 'That's top secret, I'm afraid.'

They headed away from the bright lights until, looking around, Libby realised there were few lights at all. Minutes later, he drove into a darkened and otherwise empty car park positioned one side of a quiet stretch of sand dunes. While Libby racked her brains, trying to work out what came next, her door opened and Alex offered a hand.

A cool salty breeze filed through her hair as she pushed to her feet and scanned the peaceful scene.

The hum of traffic and lights from the city seemed an eternity away while the stars were a hundred times brighter and nearer than she'd ever seen. Beyond the dunes, the rhythmic wash of waves called. Seemed that Alex heard their call too. His hand folded around hers and he gave an encouraging tug.

'Let's walk.'

Her heart flew to her throat. 'On the *beach*?'

'Sure.' He squeezed her hand. 'Slip off your shoes.'

'Alex, you know I haven't—' Her throat convulsed and she swallowed. 'I haven't...'

Cupping her face, he smiled into her eyes. 'You haven't been on a beach since your accident. Tonight, I think that should change.'

Tonight? Right *now*? 'You're serious?'

'More than you know.'

When he slipped off his shoes, Libby's breath hitched in her chest. Barefoot, he headed toward the dunes, then threw a glance back. 'You coming?'

Libby took a few deep breaths but her head still tingled with the heavy scratchings of panic. He didn't know what he was asking.

'The sand's cool and soft,' he said before lifting his nose to the air. 'I can feel the salt spray on my face.'

Closing her eyes, Libby lifted her face too. As moist briny air filled her lungs, pictures of her playing in the sand as a girl rushed up—carefree, innocent—and an unexpected urge gripped. When she opened her eyes, her pulse was thumping with the beginnings of excitement.

Do it. Just do it!

Before she could change her mind, she swept off her shoes and hurried to meet him on top of the grassy dune. Laughing, he snatched a kiss, grabbed her hand and together they navigated the downward sandy slope.

Libby found herself laughing too. Yes, the sand was cool and powder soft. It felt so good, she had to fight the impulse to fall to her knees and scoop the grains up in her arms like she used to. Should she have tried to do this sooner, or was now simply the right time? With the right person. She couldn't say that she was completely anxiety free. But with Alex walking alongside of her, his hand fitted so firmly around hers, she could handle the unease and focus on the great memories rather than the sad.

Libby's gaze slipped to Alex's thoughtful profile as he watched the waves folding in several metres away. Was he thinking of how his mother had once taken him to the beach? Was he wishing he'd been old enough to remember? Good memories mixed with sad…

Alex seemed to come back from wherever his

mind had been and glanced down at her feet. 'How's it feel?'

'Weird,' she replied, then admitted with a happy grin. 'Nice. Very nice.'

The sparkle in his eyes said he was pleased. 'Someone once told me our only restrictions are the ones we place on ourselves.'

'Carter White?' He nodded and it made sense. But, to be fair, as Alex well knew: 'Sometimes it can be a challenge to conquer them.'

Beneath a glittering stream of stars, his gaze intensified. Was he thinking of the limitations he put on himself in later life? Personal boundaries, cut-off lines he didn't want to revisit even with all his success and world acclaim?

His pace slowed and he gestured to something up ahead. 'Looks as if we're expected.'

Libby's spirits dropped. She'd thought they were alone, just them and the stars and the sea. But, yes, ahead up the beach sat a small enclosed marquee, barely illuminated by a handful of misty lights. Then the gentle strains of a symphony seemed to fade up out of nowhere. Violins, saxophones…an invisible orchestra was playing.

But as they ventured closer, it became apparent that the marquee, and immediate area, was vacant. Libby darted a look around and pricked her ears to catch any sounds of company. But Alex didn't look the least surprised or curious.

Finally coming up to speed, she set her hands on her hips. 'You organised this, didn't you?'

He only laughed. 'Guilty, Your Honour.' He moved to an ice bucket, proceeded to inspect the champagne bottle's label, then exclaimed, 'Exceptional year. But we'll open it later. For now…' After replacing the bottle, he returned to stand before her. His warm hand twined around hers, he pressed a light kiss to her knuckles, then brought their clasped hands to his lapel. 'We're going to dance.'

'Here?'

'Yes, Libby. Here. Now.' His gaze roamed her face. 'You're going to dance with me.'

Panic fisted in her windpipe. 'But the sand…it's so uneven.'

His other hand scoped around to support her back. 'I've got you.'

Libby was ready to insist. She didn't feel like dancing. Wasn't getting her on the beach after so long breaking down a big enough fence for one night? But as his gaze continued to hold hers and his confidence in her radiated out, she pressed her lips together, inhaled one big steadying breath and, sucking it up, let the music filter over her.

As the chorus of a well-known love song grew slightly louder, Alex took one step, then another, and gradually something strong and instinctive took over and Libby began to move too, stilted at first, feeling uncertain…awkward. But he continued to move along with her, then move a little faster. Next he was winding her under his arm. When he brought her back, he swayed with her again before the music segued into something more dramatic.

He rested his forehead against her. 'What do you think? Ready to go to town?'

Before she could say, 'No! Definitely not!' he did some incredible move and wound her under his arm again before dipping her Valentino style and leading her in a dramatic tango charge. Stunned— *amazed*—at any moment Libby fully expected to fall flat on her face. But although her moves were hardly smooth, she kept up. Kept up and more! When he changed direction and slid back the other way, she gave herself over to the impulsiveness of it, to the freedom. To the trust. And for the first time in years, it was true.

She lifted her face to the moon and laughed out loud.

She was *dancing*!

They danced until the night air grew too cold on her arms. Alex removed his jacket and, moving behind her, drew the warm black fabric over her shoulders. As he stood once more in front of her, she peered up into his gaze, dark grey and intense in the shadows, and suddenly the awareness of what throbbed between them, of what they'd shared in just over a day, became too much.

She thought she'd loved Scott but the feelings she had for her ex seemed childish beside the intensity of the sensations Alex brought out in her. From the first moment they'd met, he'd touched a place within her she hadn't known about. What she felt now was beyond anything she could ever have believed could exist between a man and woman. It was exhilarating. Thrilling. And way more than a little scary.

She was feeling so much so soon. For so many reasons it wouldn't be wise to let herself feel too much more.

Libby blew out a shaky breath and stepped back. She needed some space to get her whirling thoughts together, so she headed toward the water and gazed out over the dark undulating blanket of the sea. She filled her lungs with fresh briny air, not surprised that the constant crash of waves, the ocean's thunderous heartbeat, matched her own.

At her back, Alex's natural heat enveloped her and his rich voice touched her ear, spreading ripples of intense pleasure over every inch of her skin.

'You're still cold?'

Smiling, she snuggled down into his jacket and huddled back against him. 'I'm just right.'

'Are you sure? That breeze is fresh. I flicked on the heater in case.'

She angled around. Sure enough, a tall outdoor heater was set up to one side of the marquee. Its large grate was glowing red. Deep inside the softly lit tent sat a plush divan with piles of comfy-looking cushions. A fluffy white blanket lay folded at one end.

She arched a brow. 'This is all very convenient.'

Not bothering to hide a grin, he ushered her toward the divan. 'Isn't it?'

After settling back against a pile of pillows set in one corner, she waved away his offer of champagne. She only wanted to snuggle beneath that blanket and drink in the enchanting view with Alex's strength and heat supporting her.

When Alex joined her, he shook out the blanket and tucked the soft folds in. 'Warm enough?'

Burrowing into him, she sighed against his chest. 'Now I am.'

They sat together, her legs curled up to one side, the heater emitting a warm ghostly glow while the moonlit sea stretched out before them to infinity.

With her cheek resting against his chest, he was stroking her shoulder when he noted, 'The moon on the water looks like a net cast with pearls.'

She examined the sea, then sat up and gave him

a curious look. 'You really have a thing for pearls, don't you?'

He chuckled. 'Not before meeting you, I swear. Maybe it was our conversation the other day over lunch—' his palm traced over her crown '—or perhaps it's the lustre of your hair that reminds me whenever we're together.'

Libby considered his words. She supposed pearls could be the jewel for her. Diamonds sure as heck hadn't worked. The cluster she'd worn as an engagement ring had been gorgeous but had never been truly special to her, no doubt because Scott hadn't presented her with a ring when he'd proposed. After many embarrassing questions from friends and family, she'd gone and bought her own. After everything had fallen apart, she'd been so disillusioned she'd sworn never to wear another diamond on her finger. But pearls…

Yes. Maybe pearls.

But then, 'My gran used to say pearls mean tears.' Guess that suited too; she'd shed a few in her life.

'In some religions pearls represent completeness.'

She laughed. 'Is there anything you're not an expert on?'

He leaned forward and his lips skimmed hers. 'I plan to learn a lot more about you.'

His mouth slanted over hers and any chill in

the air seemed to evaporate into steam. As the temperature beneath the blanket climbed, Libby's thoughts drifted back to pearls, the mysteries they seemed to conceal, and how Alex continued to uncover so many previously depressed levels inside of her.

She trembled at the welcome pressure of his hand ironing over her bodice. Then he was delving beneath the cup, the pad of his thumb rubbing the tight aching peak and reducing her insides to liquid fire. Leaning in, she measured the broad expanse of his chest beneath his shirt, marvelling at how something as simple as feeling the crisp crinkle beneath her palm could bring out such intensely charged emotions. The invisible zip at the side of her gown came down and her breasts, and any remaining inhibitions, were freed.

As his touch brushed bare skin, remembered sensations from the night before and this afternoon transformed and condensed into a physical need, pulsing and burning until she thought she might faint from the hunger.

When he broke the kiss and urged her gently away, her nerve-endings were sizzling. She didn't want him to stop. She only wanted to feel him naked and bearing down. But when he lifted her chin, her heavy eyelids dragged open and she realised with a start where they were. Away from prying eyes but still in a public place.

And she couldn't care less.

His voice was a drugging whisper at the shell of her ear. 'Your gown will be crushed.'

'Do you think I care?'

He smiled and she tilted her weight against him until he lay back on the pillows, then she made short work of his trouser fastenings. Over the distant thunder of waves, she heard the metallic burr of his zipper easing down. Alex's chest expanded on a giant breath and, his gaze burning, he tugged off his trousers at the same time she leaned forward and dropped a lingering kiss an inch above his navel.

Her tongue wove a trail down the arrow of dark hair that led to his thighs and soon her mouth connected with that part of him that didn't know the meaning of the word *reserved*. Circling the top of his shaft with her hand, she dragged her fingers down, then looped her tongue around the hot tip twice.

His hips arched up and he clutched a sequined pillow near her head. With him braced, she slid her lips down over the head of his erection at the same time her fisted hand came back up.

'Libby…' She heard him swallow. 'This could get dangerous.'

She hummed out her approval and went down again.

* * *

After organising a late checkout from the penthouse, she and Alex spent the remainder of the day in Surfers.

Midmorning they enjoyed an ice cream in famous Cavill Avenue, where great restaurants, beach umbrellas and micro bikinis ruled. For a bit of fun, they checked out the Wax Museum, the largest in the southern hemisphere, and marvelled at the lifelike replicas of so many singers, royal members and notorious villains. Libby commented in all sincerity it shouldn't be long before they commissioned a likeness of him.

For lunch, they stopped in for some live music, a couple of thick-cut steaks and Queensland ales at the Surfers Paradise Tavern, a local icon established back in 1925 when Surfers was a small isolated town that went by the name of Elston. When someone started belting out the chorus of a famous Slim Dusty tune, everyone joined in, including Alex.

Alex was certainly a complex character—he could be alpha-annoying, inherently charming, and there were also times when he seemed so distracted and remote. But as Alex laughed and clapped and sang along with the crowd now, Libby knew this was who he wanted to be. Who he *could* be. Relaxed. Real.

Midafternoon, the limo collected them and started inland. No matter how much she begged, Alex wouldn't let on where they were going. Thirty minutes later they pulled into a magnificent rural property, with an extravagant ranch-style mansion.

Slipping out of the limo, Libby took in the spectacular far-reaching grounds. 'This is yours?'

'A friend's.'

'You want to catch up while we're here?'

'He's in Italy.'

She frowned. 'I don't understand.'

'Darren's an old driving buddy. When he retired, he missed the thrill so much, he built his own track.'

Understanding, she smiled. 'You're going to take a car for a spin.' With her watching. Frankly, she couldn't wait to see Alex in action—as long as he, and his shoulder, didn't overdo it.

'I am indeed going for a spin.' He took her hand. 'And you're coming with me.'

Libby's heart tripped over several beats. In her own car, she hated to go past 100 k's. Surfing had its dangers, certainly, but simply thinking of the kind of speeds Alex merely cruised at on a track left her mind reeling and stomach somersaulting.

She stammered and stuttered and said she couldn't possibly but, as usual, Alex wouldn't take no for an answer. And when Libby remembered the night before—walking along the beach, dancing beneath the stars—amazingly she found she could find the courage for this as well.

Ten minutes later they had donned helmets and were buckling up. The track unwinding before them looked very much like the professional circuits Libby had seen on cable. As Alex kicked in the engine, she told herself to relax and enjoy the experience. Didn't help that her knuckles had turned white, gripping her thighs.

'This here is one fast car.'

'Convertible,' she added, feeling even more vulnerable with the top down. She moistened dry lips. 'Just how fast are we going to go?'

He reached for her knee and squeezed. 'You don't want to know.'

Alex stepped on the pedal—floored it, in fact. The car flew off and Libby left a screaming laugh behind.

They went from naught to three thousand kilometres per hour in three point five seconds. Or that's how it felt. With wind blasting through her hair, scared out of her wits, Libby hung on and told herself she was not only in the hands of a professional, she was in the care of the best. Everything might be belting by in a blur. Common sense said if they crashed they would die. Just when she thought her pulse couldn't race any faster she saw the sweeping bend up ahead.

Her jaw dropping, she swung a horrified look at Alex's concentrated profile. His eyes were narrowed, his hands firm on the vibrating wheel, a smile of pure exhilaration tugged on his lips. He changed down, she held her breath and they took the turn with his foot still down. All four tyres skidded sideways, drifting around the arching corner as if they'd hit black ice.

Libby let go a wailing scream.

Over the roar of the engine and whistle of the wind, Alex heard Libby's shriek of horrified delight and, righting the car, laughed out loud.

Priceless.

It hadn't hit until this minute but he'd never been in this situation before—in a car on a track with a woman. Until today, he'd never considered the possibility. But as he gunned the 650 horsepower engine down the far straight, he realised this was a first in more than one way.

Whenever he hit a track, he was unfailingly focused on bettering himself, achieving his best, but today wasn't about career or proving anything. Not in the typical sense, in any case. He only wanted to have fun or, more correctly, he wanted *Libby* to have fun. From what he could see of the stretched smile on her face through the hair whipping around her head, it seemed he'd achieved precisely that.

By eight, they were back at Sydney Airport, where the limousine was parked ready to take them home. But Libby's mind was still spinning. The night

away had been amazing enough without that unbelievable experience on the track this afternoon. She
thought she had a good grip on who Alex Wolfe
was, but she'd only known half of it. After that
wild, hair-raising ride, she'd come to appreciate
in a way she couldn't have before what got him so
jazzed about racing and why he was fighting tooth
and nail to keep on top: to hold onto that fabulous
sense of freedom combined with the ultimate sense
of control.

Alex waited until they'd pulled up outside her
apartment block before he took her hand and said,
'Come back to Rose Bay with me.'

Wanting to so badly, she closed her eyes and
shook her head. 'That's not a good idea.'

'I think it's a great idea.'

He leaned closer—his shoulders, his mouth—
but she put both hands against his chest and explained, 'I need to be up early, and if I go back to
your house I won't get any sleep.' They were both
running on adrenaline as it was.

He seemed to think her excuse through, then
reluctantly agreed.

'In that case…' He reached into the limo's side
door pocket and retrieved a small pink plastic bag.
He looked at it awkwardly as if debating what to
do with it. Then he offered it over.

'I bought you a gift.'

She blinked first at him, then at the bag. 'What is it?'

'Open it and see.'

With an uncertain smile, she accepted the bag and slid the contents into her palm. She sighed at what she saw. A gold clamshell, the size of a dessertspoon, held a bed full of glittering light blue stones. Dotted amongst those stones sat three separate creamy beads the size of freshwater pearls. A clasp was linked to the top of the shell.

Beside her, Alex leaned close. 'I picked it up at one of those tourist stores. The blue stones symbolise the sea. The pearls represent the past, present and the future. I thought it suited you.'

Libby's heart beat high in her throat. It was a trinket, an inexpensive charm that he'd put real thought into, and she *loved* it!

Over the thickness in her throat, she murmured, 'It's perfect.' She'd never known anything *more* perfect.

He curled some hair away from her flushed cheek. 'I'll walk you up.'

She lowered the charm. It had been an incredible couple of days but she couldn't think about saying goodnight to Alex at the building entrance or her apartment door. He might suggest coming in and, the way she felt now—the way she'd felt all weekend—she wouldn't be able to turn him away. Tonight she needed to.

'If you walk me to the door,' she said, 'you'll kiss me and, before I know it, I'll be tugging you inside. We both need some sleep.'

His brow furrowed and a muscle in his jaw flexed twice but finally he nodded and knocked on the glass partition, signalling the driver to collect her luggage and open her door.

'Thank you for a wonderful weekend,' she said, her heart so full she thought it might burst.

'We'll do it again soon.'

But he didn't mention specifics…didn't mention the wedding…and after an all-too-brief kiss goodnight, the driver opened her door and carried her luggage to the building entrance. She let herself in, heard the purr of the limo's engine as it pulled out from the curb, then she gazed down again at the pearl charm in her hand. If not for this, she might think it was all some fantastic dream.

Feeling so churned up inside, she held her stomach. Before this weekend she'd known Alex was scorching. Now she found his company positively irresistible and for way more reasons than his looks and his charm. Everything she'd learned about him…everything she'd confessed about herself…

Alex Wolfe was a complex person. A world-renowned celebrity. A man who had helped her face some fierce, long-held fears. He was more than any woman could hope for and Libby simply couldn't deny it any longer.

She was falling in love.

CHAPTER ELEVEN

THE next morning, Libby dragged herself into her office. She felt groggy. Not surprising given her lack of sleep the night before. After tossing and turning till dawn, in hindsight, it might have been easier if Alex *had* walked her to the door. At least she wouldn't have woken up lonely.

Instead she'd placed the pearl charm on her bedside table and had lain awake watching the imitation jewels sparkle in the moonlight while going over every moment of her amazing weekend with Alex Wolfe...her client. Her lover.

The superstar sportsman with the shoulder she'd agreed to put through a thorough examination two days from now.

If she found him unfit to drive, Alex had said he'd take her to that family wedding. But he hadn't mentioned it last night when he'd dropped her home. He was banking on his injury passing her assessment. And if she found his joint needed more time to heal… The former athlete in her said he wouldn't take the news well.

But she couldn't give him a green light simply to make him happy, she told herself, crossing her office's reception area. And if he was half the man she'd come to believe him to be, even if he were unhappy, Alex would understand her position. He might be upset with the situation but he wouldn't be angry. At least, not with her.

Behind her desk, Payton glanced up. Her mouth rounded before she dropped her head and disappeared behind the counter's top lip.

Libby looked around. Had she missed something?

'Payton…everything all right?'

Peering back over the counter, Payton gave a coy look. 'How was your, uh, weekend?'

'My *weekend*?' Libby's stomach flip-flopped twice. 'How did you know—?'

Then she saw a celebrity magazine open on the desk and the half-page shot of her and Alex checking in at the casino Saturday afternoon. All her strength funnelled through her middle and out her toes. Baby-fawn weak, she let the counter help hold her up while she croaked out, 'Is that the only picture?'

'In *this* magazine. There was another one out on Friday.'

From her desk's top drawer, Payton slid out

another magazine, folded to a page, to a snap, of Alex and some unidentifiable female he was kissing in the entrance of an apartment block.

Looking uncomfortable, Payton wriggled back in her seat. 'I'm guessing the woman Alex Wolfe's kissing is you.'

Libby remembered Alex's hesitation on the Manly esplanade on Saturday morning when he'd noticed a small group studying him. She remembered that one of the group had held a magazine. Now she knew what had amused them so much: they'd seen her and Alex walking together and were speculating on whether he was really *the* Alex Wolfe and if she was the woman in the photo.

Slipping against the counter edge, Libby held her woozy head. This was worse than she'd ever imagined. As Payton suggested, it wasn't certain who the woman in that kissing photo was but it wouldn't be hard to put two and two together after this additional *clearer* shot taken on the Gold Coast.

She'd known this kind of a leak was a possibility and yet she'd gone ahead and continued to see him intimately anyway. Now the stark reality glared out at her. If she gave Alex what he wanted on Wednesday after her evaluation, who would believe she hadn't been charmed or, worse, bribed?

She slipped her bag, holding the pearl charm,

behind her back and muttered as she headed off, 'I'm unavailable for calls.'

But Payton wasn't letting her friend off that easily.

'Libby, please. Talk to me. This is so *huge*. I mean…ohmigod…Alex *Wolfe*!' She held her heart as if it were pounding and said solemnly, 'I bet he's an unbelievable kisser. Did you ever think for one moment that he'd fall for you like this?'

Libby stopped, shuddered and walked haltingly back. Maybe there were some photos she hadn't seen yet. Good Lord, she hoped there hadn't been any telescopic lenses pointed at the beach that night!

'I was telling my friend, Tawny,' Payton went on, 'that when he was here the other day I thought he was looking at you with a real sultry gleam in his eye. And then when you didn't come back from lunch at all that day, I didn't want to say anything but my imagination went through the roof—'

'*Payton*.' Feeling her entire body erupt in a blush, Libby threw a worried glance toward the front entrance. 'I don't want you spreading gossip like that.'

Payton's eyebrows slanted in. She looked confused. Hurt. 'But, Libby, *everyone* knows. It's all over the papers and the internet. What's wrong? If I were you, I wouldn't give a tinker's tap what the press is saying.'

Her knees gone to jelly, Libby had slumped against the counter. The internet? She felt gutted. No. She was *numb*.

Libby stumbled into her office, fell into her chair and, holding her flushed cheeks, groaned. Once upon a time she'd thrived on publicity. In her day, she'd adored being Australia's poster girl. She'd been on fire, but she wasn't so hot anymore, and a huge diversion from Alex Wolfe's usual female fare. He had a reputation for seeing starlets and supermodels and positively no one who came close to resembling her. The press would try to crucify her.

But strangely she didn't care about that aspect. She knew how Alex felt about her. How he saw her and had helped her see herself that way again too. She might have given back mobility and strength to his arm but he'd given back infinitely more.

A scratching on the window had Libby swinging around. Through the glass she caught the fervent expression of a man with shaggy coffee-coloured hair before the flash of a professional camera went off and blinded her. Shielding her eyes, she lunged over and snapped shut the blinds at the same time Payton flew through the doorway.

'Libby, a reporter's in the foyer.'

A person was on Payton's heels. Peering over her shoulder, the young man with silver framed eyeglasses held up a mini recorder. 'I'm after a quote, Ms Henderson. People want to know about Alex Wolfe's latest love interest.'

For an instant, rather than the reporter, Libby saw Alex standing there as he had almost a week ago when he'd asked her to lunch and she'd taken that first step toward her ordinary life being turned on its head. She loved being with Alex, but she wanted no part of this.

While Payton tried to crowd the reporter back, Libby struggled to assemble her thoughts, but the intruder was beyond eager to snare this ripe opportunity.

'You were Female World Surfing Champ years ago, Libby. Do you have any comment on your accident? Does Alex know that you wear a prosthesis? Do you compare yourself to the women Alex Wolfe usually dates?'

Growling, Payton grabbed the reporter's arm and tried her best to wrestle him out. But when Libby came steadily forward, the two stopped their battle, the reporter clearly anticipating a gossip worthy response.

'You'd like a reply,' Libby asked, and the reporter nodded. So she first held the doorjamb for ballast, swung back a leg and kicked him as hard as she could in the shin. When he jumped and howled, she announced, 'That's my answer.'

Payton gave an astonished way-to-go look before Libby closed and locked the door.

Libby listened to her friend herding the reporter away while delayed tears threatened to rise. The reporter hadn't said anything new...about her accident...her leg...most particularly the fact that it seemed an anomaly that a man like Alex Wolfe should find her appealing. *Sexy*. Scott certainly hadn't after that day.

But they were different men. Different on so many levels.

Her cell phone rang. She reached her bag and retrieved the call at the same time she saw the screen blink out the caller's name. Alex Wolfe.

'Are you available for lunch?' he said down the line. 'There's a restaurant I want to take you to but it's difficult to get a reservation. I wanted to call early.'

'You know about those magazines, don't you?' she asked straight out.

The silence on the line finally ended in an expulsion of air. 'Yes.'

'That's why you phoned. To see if I knew too.'

He exhaled again. 'I'm sorry, Libby.'

'It's not your fault,' she said. 'It was bound to happen. I knew that as well as you did.'

'You're okay with it?'

Libby thought about the photographer scratching at her window, the reporter barging into her office and asking the rudest questions. But she wouldn't tell Alex what that obnoxious man had said. No doubt the press would do all they could to ask Alex the same.

What did he find appealing about a cripple like Libby Henderson?

'Libby?'

'I'm fine,' she said, then took a breath and told herself that she was. She'd weathered worse. She'd survive. 'I'll be over by nine for our session but I can't go to lunch.'

'Can't or won't?'

'Alex, we have some intense days ahead of us. Let's concentrate on that.'

His voice deepened. 'You're sure you're okay?'

She said yes but wanted to add, *Or I will be.*

She couldn't wait for Wednesday to come and go. She knew Alex couldn't either.

She and Alex worked diligently together on Monday and Tuesday. She told him she'd feel happier not to see each other on an intimate basis until these hard yards were out the way. They didn't discuss those photographs again. He didn't mention whether any reporters had tried to get a quote. She couldn't bear to go near her computer or the internet and told Payton to do her a favour and not fill her in on any goss.

When Wednesday dawned, Libby rocked up at the Rose Bay mansion and tested Alex's shoulder. She held nothing back and was vigilant for any sign of weakness or pain, but he showed no trace of fatigue. Never came near wincing. After their setback on Friday, she found it difficult to believe. She didn't want to make a mistake or have anyone assume she'd forfeited her ethics for her 'boyfriend.' Her client's best interests always came first. And in this case, it seemed, Alex's interests would be best served by returning early to the track.

Of course the team doctor would want to perform his own evaluation. But she couldn't see that he wouldn't concur. Seemed Alex Wolfe would be racing in China after all. Hopefully he would surge back to the top, and her reputation would be left intact. Of course they wouldn't be attending his brother's wedding, but she had a feeling that with the eldest brother's unexpected appearance after twenty years, there would be many more Wolfe reunions in the future. Hopefully she and Alex would continue to see each other…which meant her privacy would be affected. She could barely tolerate the thought of being corralled by heartless members of the paparazzi as she had been on Monday. But it was a price she was prepared to pay.

With the evaluation complete, Alex shrugged back into his shirt. 'Well, doc, what's the verdict?'

Standing alongside him before the mirror, she crossed her arms and raised her chin. 'I have to say that based on what I've seen today and the progress that you've made…'

He stopped buttoning and almost frowned. 'Is it a green light or a red?'

She smiled. 'Green. In my opinion your shoulder is strong enough to cope well under professional car racing conditions.'

Ecstatic, Alex punched the air, but he was wise enough to do it with his left arm. Then he brought her close and kissed her with a tender passion that left her heart banging against her ribs. When his mouth released hers, he smiled into her eyes and then, relieved and so pleased, he laughed and Libby discovered she was laughing too. She'd made the right decision, and now she only had to wait for Alex to win that race in Beijing and then contact her to discuss how, where and when they would celebrate. The world might see her as 'not up to par' but Alex wouldn't use her emotions, use her growing affection and trust, to get what he needed. Not after everything they'd shared.

Alex strode over to collect his phone off a ledge near the treadmills. 'I need to call the team manager. The test driver needs to be told and forms have to be signed.'

Understanding completely, Libby headed off to collect her bag. 'Absolutely. I'll be on my way.'

Phone in hand, Alex quizzed her eyes. 'Do you need to write up a letter? Sign something?'

'I'll fix it with your assistant when I get back to the office.'

He held her gaze, his expression lighter than she'd ever seen, but somehow she knew he wasn't really seeing *her*. Rather he was imagining the crowd cheering him on this weekend. He was anticipating the challenge and thrill of being back in the driver's seat, of doing what he was born to do. Race and win. He was excited. He had every right to be.

Of course he'd need to keep up with the specific stretches and strengthening exercises, not only for the short-term but for the rest of his life. He'd need regular physio checkups to be on the safe side. Given he wasn't permanently stationed here in Sydney, it didn't necessarily have to be her.

Libby chewed her lip.

How much time did Alex actually spend in Australia?

As if he'd read her thoughts, Alex set the phone aside and strode over. Looking proud and happy, but also distracted, he held her upper arms and spoke in an earnest voice she hadn't heard before.

'We can celebrate next week. In the meantime… can you fly out later today?'

She could only gape. *Fly out?*

'You mean to *China*?'

'Practice laps start tomorrow.'

Libby held her swooping stomach. She couldn't get her mind around what he'd asked. She'd assumed that he'd board his private jet and, focused only on the finish line, leave her behind. He wanted her to fly with him to Asia?

But, 'I—I can't. I have appointments.'

Responsibilities. He knew that.

His mouth pressed into a thin line. 'There's no use trying to convince you, I suppose. But I can be back by Tuesday. We'll go out on the town then.'

Holding that thought, she nodded, snatched a kiss and, grinning, headed for the door. 'Great. Then I'll leave you with it.'

'I'll see you out.'

'No. Really, I'm fine.'

But he was already a step ahead of her.

As they walked down the hall, she tried not to dwell on the fact that he didn't take her hand or rest his palm against her back as he had these past days. His mind was thousands of miles away. Understandable. She remembered well how intense psyching up before a competition could be.

After opening the front door, he accompanied her out on to the patio. Suddenly uncertain of whether to kiss him again, shake his hand or perhaps simply send a salute, she muttered a quick, 'Good luck,' then headed for the steps. About to take the first, a hand on her elbow pulled her up.

She turned and peered up into his smiling eyes. 'One more kiss and I'll let you go.'

He was bringing her near when Libby's thoughts leapt upon those intimate shots taken of them last week. Then she thought of those horrible questions that reporter had shot at her, and she flinched and pulled away.

'Let's not.' She skipped a glance around. 'There could be some lenses pointed this way.'

But, smiling still, he only slid a step closer so Libby took a step back. Then the ground seemed to vanish from beneath her and she was falling backward with nothing to grip. Her arms had flailed in an arc over her head and her body was going horizontal when her waist was lassoed and she was tugged back up and onto her feet.

Out of breath, she got her balance, then her bearings. She looked over in time to see Alex's right arm fall away from its hook around the nearby patio column…in time to see him grimace and hold his shoulder while his jaw clenched tight. When he saw her studying him, his hand dropped away, the contorted expression vanished and he rolled back his shoulders.

Holding her roiling stomach, she came closer and reached to touch the joint. 'Oh, God, Alex, you're hurt.'

Winding away, he seemed stuck between a scowl and a smile.

'I'm *fine*.'

'Please, Alex, let me see.'

He caught her hand. 'You were on your way to write a letter.'

'Are you in much pain?'

'Not even a twinge.'

She studied his darkening gaze and swallowed back worry and regret. Her voice was choked. 'I'm sorry—' sorrier than he could ever imagine '—but I don't believe you.'

His eyes narrowed at the same time his nostrils flared and a vein pulsed down the side of his throat. 'You want proof?' He fisted his right hand and brought it almost level to his waist before bringing it down again. Dying inside, Libby bit her lower lip. He hadn't been able to lift his arm any higher.

She put a professional note in her voice. 'We'll get another MRI.'

'No more tests, dammit! I'm ready to drive.'

'I'm sorry, Alex, I'm so sorry.' She knew what it meant to him. What he thought he was losing. *Everything.* 'But I don't think you are ready.' She raised her hands in a calming gesture. 'We'll work on it, okay? Your next race after China is when? Two weeks? If we put all our effort into—'

'Right now I need to make a phone call,' he cut in, something like rage and betrayal darkening his face. 'If you'll excuse me.'

He turned on his heel and left Libby gaping as the door shut in her face.

At one in the afternoon, Eli Steele arrived at Libby's practice. Payton led him straight through to her office.

Eli was a tall, attractive man. Well-mannered, Libby remembered as she rose from behind her desk. And one hundred and ten percent dedicated to Alex Wolfe. She wondered if Alex had ever abused his assistant's trust like he'd so recently abused hers. Having that twelve-foot-high door shut in her face wasn't an event she'd soon forget.

'I have communication here from Alex,' Eli said, after taking her hand in a professional greeting. 'I wanted to deliver it in person.'

Her stomach churning, Libby murmured that she appreciated that and with shaking hands opened the sealed envelope. Holding her breath, she scanned the lines.

> *Libby,*
> *Thank you for all your efforts. After discussions with my team manager and doctor it's been decided my situation may well benefit from a different approach. I thank you for your time and dedication to date. I will be in contact after I'm back behind the wheel.*
> *Sincerely, Alex Wolfe*

Feeling as if a bomb had exploded in her face, Libby set down the letter.

'He's…disappointed,' Eli explained, as if that could be an excuse.

Alex was disappointed?

She sank into her chair. 'So am I.'

Particularly that he'd had Eli do his dirty work. Bet it wasn't the first time.

Like a good assistant, Eli made an excuse. 'You have to understand…racing is Alex's life. He couldn't be a champion if he didn't concentrate everything he had on showing up and winning.'

But she was still digesting the brevity and formal tone of that note. *I thank you for your time and dedication to date.*

Her fingers balled up the paper.

Where did he come off thinking he could treat her, treat *any* woman, this way? Three days ago they were together, laughing, racing around that track at incredible speeds. Making love. *Sharing!*

Swallowing the hurt and disbelief, she set the note aside. 'You can tell Mr. Wolfe that I expected more from him…but I shouldn't have. I hope you don't mind me saying, Eli, neither should you.'

Alex cared only about himself—his career—and he would use anyone for any purpose to get what he needed to get to and stay on top.

Eli rearranged his feet. Nodded at the ground.

Then he blew out a breath and headed out. 'Good luck, Libby.'

Libby was still sitting, getting more incensed by the second, when Payton edged in and closed the door.

'Want to talk about it?'

'I was an idiot,' Libby admitted, her face unbearably hot. 'I did precisely what I swore I wouldn't. I got involved with a client—and not just *any* client.'

She remembered Alex reaching to kiss her and how, worried about photographers, she'd pulled away. He must know, above all else, she only wanted his shoulder to mend. This morning had been a terrible accident. Like his spin-out on the track. Like her incident in the surf. But that didn't help, did it?

She should have stuck to the original plan, the one that would've worked for everyone. She should have kept their relationship professional, no matter the temptation. Instead she'd let herself be charmed, then dumped like an old pair of jeans.

She glared at the bunched note.

She'd never told Scott how little she'd thought of his behaviour toward her after her accident. Years on she wasn't so magnanimous. How dearly she wanted to teach this particular pompous ass a lesson in decency.

On returning from Rose Bay this morning, she'd

told Payton everything. Payton had hugged her for a long time. Now her friend hugged her again.

'Libby, this wasn't your fault. You're only human.'

Libby groaned. 'Seems Alex doesn't have that problem.'

How would he have acted if she hadn't signed off on his injury after the evaluation this morning? Would he have closed the door in her face anyway, as he'd done after he'd caught her on the porch?

Feeling ill, she leant back in her chair and stared blindly at the ceiling.

She had to face facts. He'd used her. She wasn't inadequate as the press had depicted. It was worse.

She was an outright fool.

CHAPTER TWELVE

Two weeks later, standing in the pits in Catalunya, Spain, Alex watched over his team as they ran their battery of checks on his car's precision instruments.

He usually got off on the noise of the pits...tools clanging, crews conversing, motors revving. The smell of oil and rubber and elbow grease was normally a great stimulus. The anticipation of feeling tyres gripping asphalt as he zipped around another competition track was a huge buzz. Alex thought he'd never grow tired of it.

And yet today those much loved highs were noticeably absent. In fact, his gut was mincing, and not with its usual healthy mix of pre-performance nerves and adrenaline. His malady wasn't because he didn't believe in his ability, he decided, heading toward the team manager, who was watching a sequence on a monitor at the rear of the pit. He would not only race this weekend, he would *win*. He'd made sure he'd set Libby Henderson well outside

his radar so he wouldn't have that distraction playing on his mind. No way did he need to combat the
same kind of turmoil he'd endured before charging
out at the track before his accident.

Six weeks on, he'd digested all the family news.
Jacob had returned to the scene and was working to
restore old Wolfe Manor. According to Annabelle's
latest communication, Nathaniel was happy and
married to his new bride. She'd even sent photos
of the day. Sebastian's five-star hotel—the London
Grand Wolfe—was certainly something.

And Annabelle...

Frowning, Alex remembered Libby's question
about whether brother and sister had ever discussed
that tragic night. For twenty years he'd managed
to keep those thoughts—his sense of guilt—from
intruding on his life too much. And yet lately, the
more he thought about that time, the more the fact
that he'd never had the courage to look Annabelle
in the eye afterward niggled the hell out of him.
The real kicker was that in his heart he'd always
known that by avoiding her gaze, brushing the
subject under that mat, he'd only hurt her more.

His focus wandered over to the recording that
the team manager was watching on the pit monitor.
He recognised the track, the car. He sure as hell
remembered the crash. Alex shuddered. He understood everyone was eager for that kind of incident
never to occur again. Every factor leading up to, as

well as the accident itself, would be mulled over and dissected again and again in a bid to avoid a repeat performance. But, dammit, he couldn't bear to watch it even one more time.

As he pivoted away, that tendon in his shoulder twinged again. He hid his flinch, then slid a casual glance around. No one had noticed. Cupping the joint, he rotated his arm and felt the faint ache again, just for a second. His strength in his injured shoulder was so much better than it had been two weeks ago. Still, every now and then...

Deep in thought, Alex moved out toward Pit Row.

Morrissey has been in communication with the replacement physio Alex had hired, and was happy with the subsequent report. After his own examination, Morrissey had cleared Alex for this round. Jerry Squires, however, had offered a stinging remark. 'If your shoulder doesn't hold up because of the incident with that woman, I'll sue for malpractice.'

Alex hadn't been certain which incident the team owner meant. Libby's fall, which Alex had caught and the new physio had reported on, or the affair?

Either way, no matter how their relationship had ended—and it hadn't ended well—Alex would never allow Libby to be hurt because of him. He'd hurt her enough already by refusing to see her. By saying goodbye with nothing more than a note. After what they'd had together, she must despise the sound of his name.

Alex pushed those thoughts aside as his ears pricked to a different kind of hype. Before a major competition, certain members of the public were permitted down Pit Row to see, firsthand, their favourite teams and drivers prepare for the big day. Rotating the arm again, Alex moved outside and scanned the clutches of people. His attention hooked on a particular boy, perhaps twelve or thirteen, wearing a shirt sporting Alex's team logo. When the boy recognised the World Number One, he bounced on the spot and his face split with a smile that warmed Alex's heart to its core.

Remembering a time he'd been that young and enthusiastic, Alex came forward.

'You like racing?' he asked the boy.

'*Muchas. Sí.*' He translated into English. 'Very much.'

Smiling, Alex nodded. 'What's your name?'

'Carlos Diaz.'

'When you grow up, you'd like to race?'

Carlos's dark eyes flashed and his little chest puffed out. 'I want to be like you. Brave. Smart. The best there is, *señor*!'

His mother patted the boy's dark head and apologised. '*El chico*, he has no father, but he has his dreams.'

Lowering his gaze, Alex remembered back and murmured, 'Reaching for dreams is what keeps us alive.'

The boy beamed at him—all faith and pride and resolve—and a shiver chased over Alex's skin as he was taken back to a time when he'd raced through the Oxfordshire countryside, chasing wild dreams with no one of patience or knowledge to guide him. Then Alex felt that homemade medal resting in his pocket, heavy as it never had been before.

Thoughtful, he fished the medal out and examined the tarnished surface of his most prized possession. The rough-hewn circle had become so much a part of him; Alex had believed he would carry it to his grave. This medal represented the opening of his gate. His escape. A new beginning. But maybe after all this time…

As he weighed the medal in his palm, his gut knotted and his fingers reflexively curled over to make a fist. But then an odd sense of calm settled over him, like a friendly hand squeezing his shoulder or patting his back, and exhaling, smiling, he reached out his hand to the boy.

'This might not look like much,' Alex said, revealing the medal again, 'but for me, it's worked miracles. It represents hope and determination and most of all it's about belief. Belief in yourself.' His opened hand nudged nearer. 'I want you to have it, Carlos.'

The boy's eyes bugged out. A heartbeat later he exploded into a barrage of animated Spanish. His mother was beside herself, holding her brow and thanking Alex repeatedly too. A sense of relief—and right—washed over him.

Alex clapped the boy's shoulder, then ruffled his hair.

'I'll have my assistant come over and get your contact details. Let's see if we can get you started.' He held up a warning finger. 'But first you'll need to learn everything there is about cars. You need to learn to appreciate their power.'

Then you can learn to harness and direct your own.

Carlos grabbed Alex's hand and pressed his mouth to the knuckles. '*Gracias, gracias*, Señor Wolfe.'

As he walked away, first to find Eli to have him speak with the boy, then to the team manager to relay his decision about stepping aside, Alex faced the cold hard truth of what he had done and immediately found peace with it.

He might want to tell himself different, but he was less than a hundred per cent fit to drive. He might be fit enough in the future. He couldn't know that for certain. What Alex *did* know was that he was able and willing to face that reality, look it in the eye, no matter how uncomfortable. And Libby Henderson had helped him do that.

After such a horrendous start, he was grateful for the significant life racing had provided. Grateful for his fans and his sponsors. But today he understood there was more. So much more. Question was…

After what he'd put her through, would Libby ever let him reach out and claim it?

CHAPTER THIRTEEN

WHEN Libby's cell phone rang, she reached to pick up. Then she saw the ID and her hand snatched back.

She had no appointments this morning. She'd told Payton she'd be in late—her bookkeeping needed attention and she could do that away from the office. After dressing, she'd packed up her laptop, took a walk and had ended up here, at the café where she and Alex had breakfast together those weeks before. She'd ordered pancakes and had forced her mind upon work. Too much time had been wasted on the frustrating question of Alex Wolfe.

Whenever thoughts of the weekend they'd spent together seeped in, she thrust them away. Two weeks on, those couple of days simply didn't seem real. If she hadn't kept the magazine shots and pearl charm, she might think that time with Alex was nothing but some fantastic dream.

The public must have thought so too. After the

day that obnoxious reporter had hounded her, the paparazzi's interest had died. Instinct must have told them there wasn't an ongoing story and instinct was right.

So why was Alex calling now? What did she have that he could possibly want? After the way he'd treated her, she sure as hell wanted nothing from him.

By the time her mind stopped spinning, the phone had quit ringing, and the smell of coffee and natter of early-morning café patrons filtered back. With a pulse drumming in her ears, Libby retrieved the message. As she listened to the rich timbre of his voice, her head began to tingle and, after a time, she remembered to breathe.

Alex wanted her to come to his Rose Bay home. He was there, waiting for her now. He could send a car if she preferred. Then his voice deepened and he said that he was sorry for the way he'd behaved, the way he'd dismissed her when she'd obviously felt so bad about what had happened.

Libby's back went up.

He was sorry?

So he *should* be.

But then she wondered. Today, Friday, was the first qualifying round in Spain. In the paper, on the sports news, everyone had been saying that Alex Wolfe was back and ready to take pole position this Saturday in Catalunya. And yet he was here in Sydney?

Libby quarrelled with herself for another ten minutes before she packed up, slid into her car and drove to Rose Bay with her fingers clenching the wheel and her heart in her throat the whole way. If he wanted to see her, hey, she wanted to see him too, but not for let's-kiss-and-make-up time, if that's what he expected. She could think of only one reason for Alex being here rather than in Spain. He'd re-injured that shoulder during practice and had decided to reinvest in his original blindly trusty physio. To even *think* he believed she would roll over and do his bidding after the way he'd cast her off made her blood boil.

When she pulled up at his lavish home, memories of that fateful first day resurfaced. Unbelievably, the nerves mixing in her stomach were even worse today. But that wouldn't stop her from finally giving Alex a piece of her mind. He'd better have hold of his seatbelt.

Stealing herself, Libby moved up those front steps, pressed the doorbell and, counting her heartbeats, impatiently looked around. About to press again, the door fanned open. She thought she was prepared for this meeting, but standing framed by that soaring doorway, Alex looked so regal and fresh and handsome and...

Near.

Coming back, Libby straightened and balled up her hands. She would *not* let herself be distracted. She had a score to settle—an ego to cut down to size—and this was the time to do it.

Libby nodded a cool greeting. 'How are you, Alex?'

'I'm good. Great actually.' With his usual casual grace, he stepped aside. 'Please, come in.'

'I thought you'd be busy on the track,' she said with remarkable poise as she skirted around and moved inside.

As he shut the door, she turned, ready to tell him that if his shoulder was still troubling him, he had better find someone else because she was no longer available. And if purple pigs had begun to fly and he was after some female companionship, he could wind out his string and go fly a kite. But before she could start, Alex was explaining about Spain.

As they stood in the massive foyer's soft fans of light, he recalled the excitement in the Spanish pits and how his team manager had watched and re-watched his spectacular crash. He admitted that, although his shoulder had been cleared in time for Spain, at the last moment he accepted that his current weakened condition wouldn't do his team any favours. And so, unbelievably, he'd stepped aside from racing until further notice. Then he described a young boy he'd met in Pit Row. A boy who dreamed of racing and being just like his hero, Alex Wolfe.

Despite her agenda, as Alex's story unfolded, Libby found herself absorbed.

'I gave Carlos, that boy,' he explained, 'my medal from Carter White.'

Libby's head kicked back. The medal his mentor had made and given him all those years ago? It meant so much to Alex. She couldn't accept that he'd handed it over to a stranger.

'But why?' she asked.

'It was time.'

'Time for what?'

'To accept the past and move ahead with my future.'

He said this boy, Carlos, had no father. Alex had set up a personal sponsorship to help with the boy's education and passion for cars. While he was on sabbatical he intended to scout for more talented teens who could use a little help.

When he took her hand, Libby was so taken aback by all she'd heard, she lacked the presence of mind to pull away.

'I came back, Libby. I've missed you.' He searched her eyes. 'I was hoping that you'd missed me too.'

He looked at her with such intense emotion. With obvious desire. But instead of being moved the way he so obviously hoped she would be, all the feelings she'd unintentionally put on the back-burner since stepping into this house came bubbling up in a thick hot rush. Tears prickled behind her eyes. How dare he lay all that on her, then tell her that he missed her, as if he hadn't discarded her so callously before he'd left. As if he truly cared.

'You haven't mentioned the note you had Eli deliver to me,' she said, struggling to keep her voice level. She was angry. Hurt. And, dammit, justified in feeling that way.

He looked sheepish. 'I needed to get back on track.'

'Pity you didn't quite manage it.'

His eyes flashed before he stepped closer and she had to arch her neck to look into his stormy gaze. 'Don't you understand what I'm telling you? Don't you know why I'm here?'

'Not to have me work on your shoulder?' she mocked.

His brows drew in. 'Of course not.'

'Then I'm guessing you'd like to sleep with me again.'

'Don't reduce it to that,' he growled.

Emotion swelled and clogged her throat. 'You shut the door in my face,' she ground out, 'flicked me away like a fly, and you honestly think I'll throw my arms around you now?'

'I said I was wrong,' he stated. 'I apologised.'

She glared at him, then turned to leave.

Apology not accepted.

But he caught her wrist. When her fiery gaze met his, his expression was set, assured...and at the same time wary.

He almost smiled. 'You don't want to go.'

'You don't know what I want.'

'Then I'll tell you what *I* want.'

He scooped her close, and before she could think to wind away, his mouth was covering hers and all the nights she'd spent dreaming of him, all the times she'd wanted to cry, came leaping up. He'd left her. She'd thought he was never coming back, and yet here he was, holding her, kissing her, telling her that...

That he still wanted her.

She didn't want to kiss him back. She wanted to break away. *Run* away. She had more self-respect, more moral strength, than this.

But as the kiss deepened, and the flames licking at her veins multiplied and spread, gradually, somehow effortlessly, she felt her arms lift, circling and helping to press her body against his. If this was a dream, God help her, she never wanted to wake up.

An eternity later, the kiss ended softly but the heat of his lips remained close. He murmured one simple word.

'Stay.'

Her heart squeezed. Despite everything she

knew and feared, she wanted to. But she couldn't. She couldn't let her heart railroad her head when she knew later she'd regret it. She shouldn't have kissed him back. She should never have come. She dropped and shook her head.

'No.'

He folded hair back from her face. 'What's stopping you?'

'Sanity,' she said. 'Pride.'

'They're both overrated.'

She gave into a grin but then swallowed it back down. 'Dammit, Alex, I'm not supposed be amused. I'm supposed to be—'

But when his lips grazed hers, the tail of that thought evaporated as a tingling wondrous thrill ripped through her. The final bricks of that wall crumbled and fell, and any remaining doubt or annoyance were replaced by an energy of a different kind—an awareness so consuming and overpowering that the battle was all over.

She was lost.

Taking soft slow kisses, he kneaded her upper arms, making her blood heat and hum. He'd missed her.

She sighed against his lips.

She'd missed him more than air.

Seconds melted into scorching minutes. As he gathered her closer, she ironed her palms over his shoulders, his chest. Her fingers twined around his shirt buttons while their kisses grew steamier still. With him leading her, they blindly headed for the stairs. His shirt fell halfway up, her shirt followed close behind. At the top of the stairs, breathing laboured, his mouth broke from hers long enough to smooth the pad of his thumb sensually over her lower lip, then guide her into the master suite.

The room was cool and dark and predictably large. The carpet and satin spread on the king-size bed were steely grey. The sheets were already folded down and the heavy curtains pulled against the morning sun.

He took her hand and, his eyes on hers, led her to one side of the bed before deliberately lowering his mouth to the curve of her throat. When his teeth grazed the skin, she shivered and sighed until all her breath was gone, then she arched her neck and offered more.

Their clothes came off quickly while they were standing, sitting, finally while they were caressing and writhing amongst the sheets. As he explored her every curve and valley, she gave herself over to the fantasy, only wishing it would never end. She thought she'd lost the chance to ever feel this beautiful again, and as he gently rolled her onto her stomach and traced slow hot kisses down her back, she had to be glad she'd succumbed one more time. She'd need these memories when it was time to let that harsh light back in.

By the time his mouth joined hers again, sparks were firing through her veins and that smouldering kernel of need at her core had begun to throb and burn. His body angled and covered hers, then he was filling her, moving with long measured strokes that pushed her, inch by inch, higher up that growing wave. His head dropped into her hair at the same time his hand fanned and gripped her thigh. He murmured her name and moved against her faster, until the powder ignited, the kindling went up and she was thrown a thousand leagues into the air.

Still throbbing above her, he dotted kisses over her brow, her cheek. When he shuddered one last time and exhaled on deep satisfaction, she drew her fingers around his bristled jaw and, short of breath, tipped up to feel his lips on hers one last time.

His mouth trailed her cheek, around her jaw. He murmured things close to her ear that almost had her believing that she was and would remain the most important thing in his life. When he reluctantly shifted to lie beside her, her mind set, she rolled to her side off the bed. As she reached to collect her bra and panties off the floor, uncertain of what she was up to, Alex sat slowly up.

'Don't get dressed,' he said lightly. 'If you have appointments this afternoon, just this once, cancel.'

'I don't have any appointments,' she said, fitting the bra's clasp.

He leaned over and warm fingers traced her back. 'Then lie down. I want to hold you.'

Lord, she was tempted. But it was out of the question. Alex had to know that. After what they'd shared, she didn't want to argue. Still she had to say this and say it now. Sitting on the edge of the bed, she turned and looked him in the eye.

'Alex, this won't happen again.'

His brows knitted, then he sat up straighter and ran a hand through his thick crop of hair. Finally he shook his head.

'What are you talking about?'

'Right or wrong, I love being with you. You can make me forget…*everything*. It's almost enough…' Emotion stuck in her throat and, wishing this was over, she lowered her gaze.

'Enough for what?'

'To make me forget what you did. How you treated me.'

How you used me.

'Libby, for God's sake. I did what you wanted. I wasn't sure about my shoulder so I threw it all in and came back.' He reached and gripped her hand. 'I came back to *you*.'

Who was he trying to fool? 'You shouldn't have left like that in the first place!'

'You honestly can't understand what I was going through?'

'I know what it's like to be on top,' she said, 'and then have the rug pulled out from beneath you. It's a huge shock. It hurts like hell. I *get* it.' Of course she did.

His gaze pierced hers for a heart-stopping beat, then he flung back the sheet and, in a temper, leapt out of bed.

'Don't make it sound like I'm washed up. Like I'm a has-been with nothing to look forward to.'

A surge of indignation ignited her cheeks. Of course he would see her as 'nothing.'

Clenching her jaw so hard her teeth ached, she thrust her feet through her trouser legs. She didn't need to stay here to listen to this. To Alex defending his precious title, even in the bedroom.

By the time her shoes were on, he seemed to have contained himself, although his voice was tellingly tight. 'I don't know why you can't put it behind you.'

'Same way you hope Annabelle's put it all behind *her*?'

She rotated to see his powerful silhouette seeming to grow larger against the shuttered light. A measure of her bravado slipped when he strode around the bed and, rigid with anger, loomed over her.

'I apologised, damn it. I've *explained*.' His eyes

blazed with outright frustration. 'What the hell do you *want* from me?'

She sized him up. He wasn't blind. Neither was he stupid. If he couldn't see what she wanted—what any woman in her position would want—she sure as hell wouldn't tell him.

Defiant—poised—she crossed her arms. 'I don't want anything from you.'

A pulse in his cheek beat erratically at the same time his grey eyes darkened, like twin thunderstorms about to unleash. But then the breath seemed to leave his body and, after two long torturous beats, his chin tipped up.

'You want to punish me for what I did. But, Libby, you're punishing us both.'

'Punishing? Or protecting?'

A patronising look on his face, he reached for her but she wound away. His mouth pressed into a hard line at the same time his jaw shifted. When he reached for her again, this time he didn't try for her wrist. Now he demanded her full attention. As his hands seized her upper arms, his mouth tilted on a sardonic smile.

'Don't tell me you're sorry that today happened. Don't try to tell me you really want to go.'

'You're right.' *Dear God.* 'I want to stay.'

But she couldn't forget Scott, or Leo. More so, she couldn't forget how Alex had dismissed her so heartlessly two weeks ago. Tears building in her eyes, she tried but couldn't swallow past the claw opening in her throat.

'But no matter how much I'd like for you to hold me—' *kiss me* '—I won't lay myself open to that kind of hurt again.'

The world seemed to shrink and press in on her lungs, on her heart, as the hold on her arms tightened. She wondered what he'd do next. Throw her out? Turn his back. Before her mind could grasp a third possibility, his mouth came crashing down, capturing and claiming hers without apology. Without reserve.

His caress was like a giant vacuum, devouring all memory other than the sublime sensory. As she lost herself to sensation, Alex curled over her more, driving her to surrender. Convincing her that she couldn't break free. He wouldn't allow it.

When his lips finally, grudgingly, left hers, their breathing was ragged and the room was spinning. His palms slid up over her shoulders to rest either side of her neck, and as his heavy gaze penetrated hers, she recognised the appeased certainty glowing in his eyes. His chest expanded as his focus dropped to her parted lips and his thumbs drew coaxing circles beneath her lobes.

'Now did *that* feel as if I want to hurt you?'

'I never said you wanted to,' she got out, feeling giddy. Weak. 'That doesn't mean you won't.' That you won't *again*.

His gaze hardened. 'I won't let you do this. I won't let you push me away.'

'No. You'd rather keep me hanging around until you're ready to get back to what's really important.' His only true passion. Racing.

Growling, he threw his hands away from her and made to hold his head as if legions of demons were scratching at his brain.

'Damn it, Elizabeth! Why do you have to be so *difficult.*'

'Would you rather I was more like Annabelle?' she shot out. He'd never been honest and open with her and, for whatever reason, his sister had let it slide.

His voice lowered to a dangerous pitch. 'Keep her out of it. You know nothing about Annabelle.'

'What's worse is neither do you.'

'Do not change the subject.'

As he enunciated each word, emotion filled her throat, stung her eyes, but she wouldn't keep quiet. She wasn't poor Annabelle.

'You *use* people, Alex. You'd do anything—use anyone—to keep in front of the pack. You used Carter White. You use Eli Steele. You use your fans and your team and your money to put a divider between you and your past. You set out to use *me*—'

'That's not *true*!' His roar echoed through the

room before his resolute gaze wavered and finally dropped away. 'Not after I got to know you.'

Libby slumped. But why should she feel so disappointed? Hadn't she known it all along? Then. Now. She was no more than a tool for Alex to manipulate to get what he needed.

When he sank down to sit on the edge of the bed, suddenly all the fight went out of her too. What was left was dull, deep acceptance. The realisation this was over and it needed to be. She stood and, leaving him behind, made her way down the stairs and out that door one last time.

She understood why Alex was happier living behind his safety nets. She was guilty of it too. It hurt less. But no matter how hard Alex pretended to be together—whole—the sad lonely truth was he was more damaged than she'd ever been.

CHAPTER FOURTEEN

'THOUGHT I'd find you here. Which one are you thinking of taking out?'

At the sound of Eli's voice, Alex held off throwing his third dart and turned to see his friend entering the Rose Bay backyard garage. After this morning's emotional roller-coaster ride with Libby Henderson, he could use a little uncomplicated male company.

When Libby had left earlier, Alex had been at a loss. Since he'd received that email from Annabelle weeks ago his life had been like a dodgem car race, complete with bang-ups and standstills and mind-spinning turnarounds. He'd done the right thing in Spain. He felt good about mentoring that boy. As far as pulling out of the race, given the intermittent pain in his shoulder, he'd had no choice but to step aside. He hadn't been so sure in predicting Libby's reaction to his invitation to his home. Their meeting had started off fiery. When they'd moved to the bedroom things had only got hotter. After making love he'd assumed their differences were all squared away.

Not even close.

Alex hurled the last dart and hit an inch off bullseye—not bad for left-handed. Then he ambled forward, past the old beat-up wreck in the corner, and wriggled the darts from the cork.

'I don't feel like driving.' Alex offered up the darts to his friend. 'Want a throw?'

Eli tugged his ear. 'I need to rush out and buy a hearing aid. Did you say you don't feel like *driving*? Has your arm got worse? I thought you were fine for everyday conditions.'

He gave a shrug that let Eli know that wasn't it.

Alex sat on a stool and twirled the darts between his fingers, watching the red and black feathers swirl one way, then the other, while he thought over what Libby had said…about Annabelle and Carter and Eli. He couldn't get her words out of his mind.

'Have you ever let a woman get to you?' Alex finally asked.

'Get to me?'

'You know. Get into your blood. Screw with your brain. She haunts me, Eli, and, I tell you, I'm done with it. I want her gone—' determined, he flung all three darts at the board at once '—out of my head.'

Eli pulled up a stool. 'You mean out of your heart.'

Alex stood to retrieve the darts. 'Don't talk to me about what I think you're going to talk to me about.'

'In three years, that's the first time I've heard you ramble.'

Alex grunted and, darts in hand, took up his position behind the line. 'That's her fault.'

'You're one stubborn SOB, you know that?'

'Nothing but compliments today.' He threw the darts, one, two... When the last one hit the wall, he took stock and caught Eli's eye and apologised, which he didn't do often.

'Sorry. I'm out of sorts today.'

'You've been on your own a long time, Alex.'

Halfway to the dartboard, Alex stopped and looked at his friend hard. 'You're not going all Dr Phil on me, I hope.'

'What is it about Libby that frightens you?'

'Why would I be frightened?'

'Make that terrified.'

Alex wriggled the darts out again. 'I simply know what I'm capable of.'

Or he thought he'd known.

She'd asked him if she was protecting them both and she'd had a bloody good point. He loved being with her. He couldn't imagine finding that kind of connection again. But he wouldn't pretend that he could promise anything and Libby had known it. He didn't do commitment unless it was to the track.

'If you ask me,' Eli said, 'and you did, you need to look at this from a wider perspective.'

'It's cut and dried. She wants something from me that I simply can't give.'

'Commitment. Maybe marriage.'

That's what she wanted, all right. Then, like magic, the goodbye note and door shut in her face would be forgotten. *Poof!*

Alex pointed out, 'I've known her a matter of weeks.'

'And despite that she put her reputation on the line when she agreed to that early evaluation.'

'That point is moot.'

After he'd hurt his shoulder again—catching Libby when she'd spilled off the patio—her evaluation had meant nothing. He'd had to start physio again. But he'd needed to work with someone else. He couldn't abide any more distractions. His life had become too complicated as it was.

Eli pushed up to his feet, walked around the stool and crossed his arms. 'Right. You don't want to drive. Seems like you don't want to talk. I'm sure you don't want to sit around all week wishing you could swap these toys for a chance to be with her again.' He paused to consider. 'Did you tell her you understood how she felt?'

'I'm pretty sure I showed her, Eli.'

'Did you say you were sorry? It's not so easy for us guys, I know.'

Alex was about to say yes, he'd apologised, and more than once. But then the words slipped away and he was left with the image of Libby, sitting beside him while he screeched around that private Gold Coast track. He was struck by the memories of how exhilarated and, to some extent, shaken he'd been afterward, knowing he'd never shared anything like that kind of experience before.

Wondering more, he angled his head.

Was he….could he be…in *love*? Did he *love* Libby Henderson in the forever-after way? Marriage, family, 'can I truly move on from my gritty childhood' way? She brought out emotions and admissions no one else could.

But then another image faded up…Annabelle. And the old scarred memories that he wished to Hades he could forget came crashing down again. All those years ago Annabelle had so desperately wanted to be part of his 'cool' crowd. Instead of listening to her, protecting her that night, he'd shoved her off home—shut the door in her face— and continued on with his own thing. As if it were yesterday he remembered the next morning, running from the police in that beat-up blue sedan over there, then facing the truth about the obscenities that had occurred the night before.

He'd felt responsible for so much of Annabelle's hurt and shame. If he hadn't turned her away, she wouldn't have been beaten by that worthless sod who'd dared call himself their father. Jacob wouldn't have had to bear the guilt of committing patricide, even if he was subsequently acquitted of all charges. Self-defence. He'd defended Annabelle. Defended them all. And Alex had lacked the courage to apologise to his twin for casting her off that night, for handing her over to that animal on a platter.

They all had their wounds. But was it too late to talk about it now? To give a part of himself he hadn't ever thought worth giving.

Alex dropped his head into his hands and, his chest aching, groaned aloud, 'Is it too late?'

'I don't think so,' Eli replied. 'But do it soon, mate. For both your sakes.'

After Eli left, Alex went into his office and clicked into his email account. He brought up Annabelle's address but then his gaze flicked to the phone. His sister, once so lively, was so reserved these days. She preferred a less personal form of communication but this time he needed to hear her voice, and she needed to hear his.

He punched in her quick dial, but when his stomach flipped he disconnected and dropped the phone on the desk. After such a long silence, did he want to do this? *Could* he bring up the most traumatic night of both their lives and be certain it wouldn't do more harm than good? What if she confirmed what he'd always feared most? That she hadn't forgiven him for thrusting her aside. Letting her down.

Just like he'd let Libby down.

His gut churning, Alex fell into the chair and held his brow.

These past weeks, this unease about the past had built until now he felt as if he were drowning. At this moment, it pressed down so heavily he could barely breathe. Even if Annabelle's reaction was less than accepting, he *had* to get this off his chest. He had never meant to hurt his sister.

And Libby…?

Setting his jaw, he collected the phone, punched in the quick dial again and, on tenterhooks, waited to hear if Annabelle picked up when she saw his ID.

Six rings. Seven.

A click and then…

'Alex? Is that you?'

'Annabelle.' His pent-up breath came out in a rush. 'It's good to hear your voice.'

'Do you know what time it is? What's wrong?'

He glanced at the wall clock and cursed under his breath. He hadn't considered the time difference. She'd be half asleep. His throat tightened. Maybe he ought to phone back.

'Alex? Are you all right?'

Concern had deepened her tone. If he hung up now, she might be up half the night worrying. This might feel a thousand times more difficult than it should be but, for better or worse, he was committed.

He cleared his throat, pushed to his feet and rushed a hand through his hair.

'There's something I need to say. I'd rather say it in person, but I'm afraid it can't wait.' This had waited long enough. He swallowed his fear and confessed after twenty long years.

'Annabelle, I'm sorry I wasn't there for you. I'm sorry I turned you away.'

A long silence echoed down the line before, sounding unsure, uneasy, his sister replied, 'What are you talking about?'

'That night.' The night no one ever mentioned. 'I'm sorry I was a jerk and booted you out of that party when I should have taken care of you. I'm sorry—' His voice caught and he found himself swallowing hard against the pit in his throat. 'I'm sorry I wasn't there for you afterward. I didn't know...' He exhaled and, broken, admitted, 'I felt guilty...I didn't know what to say. How to say it.'

When more silence wound down the line, a withering feeling sailed through him. He shouldn't have rung. Annabelle had built up a wall just as he had done. He had no right trying to break it down after so long. He should have left this buried—

But then he heard a snuffle, then a sigh, and a spark of hope lit in his chest.

'All these years,' Annabelle murmured, her voice soft and thick, 'I thought you were angry with me for causing so much trouble that night.'

Astounded, Alex coughed. 'What? *No*. I was never angry with you. I was angry with me.'

'We were children.' He heard the strain in her voice and imagined the glistening tears edging her eyes. 'It was nobody's fault.'

Wondering, Alex's hand tightened around the phone. Nobody's fault? Surely she hadn't forgiven their father. But something kept him from asking. William Wolfe was the monster behind all this pain, but Alex didn't want that name mentioned in this conversation. This was about him and Annabelle. About finally making it right between brother and his wounded and much loved sister.

'Can you forgive me?' he asked, trying not to flinch as his mind's eye called up that single red welt marring her still-beautiful face.

'Oh, Alex. No matter how far apart we've seemed, you're my other half. You always will be.'

His eyes misting over, Alex lowered into the chair and as he and Annabelle spoke more, for the first time in his life he knew a sense of true belonging. When he'd finished that phone call, despite knowing the time difference now, he called and spoke to his old friend, Carter White, and vowed to keep in touch.

He was finally making peace with himself and people from his past but he wouldn't rest until he had at least one other's. The person who had set this all in motion.

He'd given Libby parts of himself he'd never allowed anyone else to glimpse. But he'd given her much more than that. He'd given her his heart.

God knows he hadn't meant to. The very idea was as foreign as it was...*healing*. Although, after their argument today, he suspected Libby would rather consume hot coals than admit it, Alex more than sensed she felt the same way. He'd hurt her—deeply—just as he had Annabelle, and Libby wasn't prepared to be hurt again. He couldn't blame her. But now he knew to the depths of his soul what they could have together. What they *both* wanted and needed.

If it took the rest of his life, he wouldn't take her no for an answer.

CHAPTER FIFTEEN

'YOU amaze me, Libby. So many talents and you know your way around a hotplate as well.'

Collecting the plates from her dining table, Libby sent Payton an amused look. 'Chicken and roast vegetables aren't exactly haute cuisine.'

'It is the way you do them,' Payton said, following her friend into the kitchen.

Libby had invited Payton over for a meal, or rather Payton had suggested they go out, grab a bite, maybe catch a movie. But Libby had baulked at venturing out in public. Since breaking off with Alex last week, she'd tried her best to stay upbeat but, in truth, she hadn't felt much like company.

Friday afternoon last, she'd confided in Payton about the goings-on of that morning. How she'd confronted Alex and things had taken a left turn. Although walking away that day was the right thing to do, her sense of loss cut so deep that sometimes it hurt to breathe. Reason told her that she had everything to live for and yet she had the hardest time convincing her heart to listen. When she forced her mind on work, she felt in some ways happier, but when she was alone she couldn't help but remember and wish things had turned out differently. Payton had noticed her mood, which was why she'd prescribed some R and R tonight.

While Libby rinsed the plates, Payton put away the condiments. 'If you're not tired, I could go pick up a DVD. Or we could just talk.'

Libby appreciated the gesture, but it was getting late and they both had work tomorrow. She looked up from the running tap.

'I'm fine, Payton, honest.' She stacked the rinsed plates on the drainer. 'You go home and get some shut-eye.'

'Are *you* ready for bed?'

'I might go for a walk.'

'At this time of night?' Payton disappeared into the living room. Libby found her shrugging into her bright pink coat. 'I'll come with you.'

Libby smiled. Payton could be a little on the flighty side but her heart was big and her concern was always sincere.

'The path along the esplanade's well lit.' Joining Payton, Libby touched her friend's arm. 'I'll be fine.'

Payton's mouth pulled to one side before she let out a lungful of air. 'Well, if you're sure you don't want the company.' She lowered her gaze, then caught Libby's again. 'You know there's no one I admire more than you. You're the strongest person I know.'

Libby's throat constricted. She'd always tried to tell herself strength was what mattered. If you kept that, you could do anything. She was alive and had wonderful family and a great practice and excellent friends. One day she'd find romantic love again.

One day…

After she and Payton said goodbye, Libby packed the dishwasher, then wandered over to the opened curtains. Feeling hollow, she let her gaze trail over the moonlit waters of tonight's calm ocean. Once she'd been a mistress of those waves, and when that world had collapsed she'd knuckled down and had built another. In time this dull dead ache in her stomach would fade. Sometime in the future she would get over Alex Wolfe and his dazzling smile, his dynamite personality…the unbelievably beautiful way he made love.…

Growling at herself, Libby grabbed a light jacket and headed out to find that fresh air. She needed to get over this bout of self-pity, she decided, taking the lift to the ground floor. Maybe she ought to learn how to jog again. Nothing cleared the cobwebs and left you exhausted like a solid four-k run. And she really needed a holiday. Perhaps Thredbo. If she could dip and do the tango, there was no reason she couldn't relearn how to snow ski.

Five minutes later, she was moving down the same esplanade pathway Alex and she had enjoyed strolling along weeks earlier. The three-quarter moon smiled down, the powerful ocean breathed in and out, and yet, with all her tentative go-slay-'em plans, Libby's heart still felt horribly empty.

Stopping at a stairway leading to the beach, her heartbeat began to skip. The only time she'd felt sand between her toes since her accident had been that incredible night she'd spent with Alex. He'd forced her to face that fear and she'd conquered it. It had been a gigantic step. Would she ever have found the courage if not for him?

Libby took in a lungful of air, and another, then headed down the stairs. When she hit the uneven soft sand, she tipped sideways but not nearly enough to fall. Regaining her balance, she focused on her feet, half buried. She lowered onto the bottom step and removed her shoes.

A moment later, her toes dug into the cool powdery grains and Libby's heart flew to her throat as a thousand wonderful memories flooded her mind...of when she was a child with her family, then as a teen with the world at her feet, and finally as a woman, finding true courage again while falling in love.

Gradually she pushed to her feet, then drew the clamshell pearl charm from a pocket. As she rotated the piece in her palm, the moonlight caught the stones and threw back dazzling prisms of blue light. In some ways, at least, she must have meant something special to Alex.

Hadn't she?

A bus roared past and Libby glanced off to the road. Tonight there seemed to be more traffic than usual—family cars, lorries, motorbikes. But their noise was gradually swallowed up by the throatiest, roughest engine ever slapped together. Libby pivoted further around and peered up the street. Was someone taking their steam train for a run?

The streetlights reflected in her eyes but when she squinted and refocused, she recognised the car. Her stomach pitched. It was one of a kind and she could imagine only one person ever driving it.

Same dull powder-blue paint job. Same massive dents and scratches. She took a few disbelieving steps nearer.

Why was Alex driving that wreck?

What was Alex doing *here*, full stop!

The car swerved into a park and the volcanic rumble from its engine shut down. Libby gathered herself as a rusty door squeaked and slammed shut. Alex glanced first at the building, then, as if guided by radar, swung his gaze around. With half a football field between them, their eyes connected. The next instant he was leaping the beach wall and landing with an athletic grace and determination that left her weak. Without missing a beat, he continued his beeline to the spot where she stood.

When he stopped before her, looking larger than life and more handsome than she'd ever seen him, Libby wished she had a prop to lean against. He left her off balance. Dizzy with a flurry of emotions.

As a sea breeze tugged at his hair and his billowing shirt, she swallowed against the great lump in her throat. The question *Why did you come?* burned the tip of her tongue but she didn't feel ready to hear his response.

Instead she asked, 'Why are you driving that wreck?'

He owned so many amazing cars. That one sounded as if it were ready to cough out its last breath.

'I decided it was time to settle up with slices of my past and either unload or re-embrace them.' He jerked a thumb back at the bomb. 'I'm going to do her up again. She's still beautiful despite the beating she took. I owe it to her—me too—to make it right.'

Libby quizzed his committed gaze. There was more to what he'd said—to the expression on his face—but before she could ask, he went on. 'I didn't expect to find you down here, walking on the sand.'

She stole a glance over her shoulder, saw the tide was on its way in, and instinctively took two steps toward the road…toward Alex. And that was dangerous. Whatever he was doing here—to apologise again, to seduce her because he knew he could—no matter what her heart said, she didn't want to hear it.

'I thought you'd be in another country by now,' she stated stiffly.

Beneath the moon- and streetlight, a ghost of a smile touched his lips. 'I have business to attend to.'

'Business?'

Holding her with his eyes, he stepped closer. 'Of the utmost importance.'

With her heartbeat pounding in her ears, she managed an offhanded shrug. 'Something to do with your aftershave?'

'Something to do with you, Libby. To do with us.'

When that smile reached his eyes, her skin flashed hot. She dropped her gaze to the wet sand at her feet and held herself tight. His coming here, playing with her like this…it wasn't flattering or charming. After the way they'd parted, knowing the way she felt, this was plain cruel.

'I need to go.'

She moved to angle around him but he blocked her path.

'Libby, listen to me. *Please*.'

Trembling inside, she kept her gaze lowered on

the damp ripples left on the sand by the tide. If she peered into those soft grey depths now, he might talk her into anything.

With a knuckle he lifted her chin and, when their eyes met, his searching hers so deeply, she felt her will being sucked away.

'You said yourself. We understand each other. We appreciate each other too—' his brows nudged together '—even if there were times I didn't let you know like I should have. Maybe we wouldn't share that understanding if our lives had been spared the tragedy. I wish my childhood had been different, that my father had been a loving, caring man who had cheered me on instead of either ignoring me or trying to crush me beneath his heel. I wish I'd known my mother.' He took both her hands in his, so warm and firm. 'And you must wish that you hadn't gone into the surf that day. We've been dealt some bad cards but it's the only hand we had to play.' His arm slipped around her waist and he smiled softly. 'We're survivors. We brush ourselves off and we find a way to go on.'

A ragged breath caught in her chest. Her heart was squeezing so much her lungs hurt. And plump tears were rising, welling in her eyes. Dammit, he wasn't playing fair.

'You know how I feel about your childhood.' She wished she'd been there as an adult to have rescued them all. 'But what happened back then...' She swallowed against raw emotion. 'Alex, it doesn't have anything to do with now.'

'I think it does.' His voice lowered. 'Everyone's destined to take some wrong turns, like me suggesting at the start that you go against your conscience. Like shutting you out that day.' A pulse beat in his throat as he drew her gently near. 'That was wrong. I knew it, but I was trying to convince myself that retaining the championship was more important. I wanted to keep what I had. What I knew. But being with you…' His gaze intensified as it roamed her face. 'You've taught me there's more than wanting to drive fast cars. I've learned that I *want* more. Can *give* more. That I'm ready.'

Just as he'd asked, Libby had listened, with the wash of the waves coming closer and the hope of his words reaching mercilessly deep.

Her question was a hoarse anxious whisper. 'How much more?'

'I want it all,' he said simply. 'Marriage, kids. But only with you. I want us to have a life. Together I know we'll do it right.' His gaze dropped to her lips before finding her eyes again. 'I love you, Libby. I love you so much.'

She sucked down a breath at the same time a hot tear sped down her cheek. Was this a dream? Had she heard right?

'Are you saying…?'

'I'm asking you to marry me.' His warm lips

brushed her temple. 'God knows I can live without chequered flags. I can't live without you.'

Another tear fell, and another. He wanted her to believe in him. He *loved* her. Couldn't live without her. She wasn't sure which way to turn. What to say.

She swallowed back disbelieving, happy tears again. 'You're sure?'

'As sure as I know that together we can do anything. Go anywhere. Have everything.'

She gave in to the feelings that had haunted her these past days and, wanting so much to trust— to believe—she finally surrendered and let the words come.

'I love you too.' Her throat ached with the depth of her love. 'You can't imagine how much.'

Her words were barely out before his mouth claimed hers and every fibre in her body sparked like tinder and caught light. As his arms drew her closer still, she submitted, to his kiss, to his belief in them both. Most of all she submitted to their love.

A series of car horns, blaring from the street, brought her back. She and Alex glanced toward the road. Some young men in souped-up cars were beeping and hooting at the couple shamelessly embracing on the beach.

Laughing softly, Alex brought his gaze back to

hers, then cocked a brow. 'You know what this means, don't you?'

'We'll probably wind up in tomorrow's newspaper?'

'In that case, let's give them something to talk about.'

His left arm hooked under her legs and then her feet were swinging in the air and she was cradled firmly against his chest.

She gasped. 'Be careful! Your shoulder.'

'I'm strong enough for this.'

When he moved toward the water, Libby's blood pressure dropped and she stiffened to a board. *'What you are doing?'*

'Don't worry. We'll do it together.'

'You mean go into the water? *Now?*'

'Do it this once,' he said, 'then, if you want, you can put it behind you.'

Her head began to prickle. She broke out in an all-over sweat. 'I…I *can't.*'

But he began moving again, then she heard his feet swishing through the water and felt the cool spray of the sea on her skin.

'I'll keep you safe,' he said. 'From this moment on I'll always be here for you. I'll never turn away.'

Carefully she laced her arms around his neck but gasped when her foot swept through the cool wet.

Concerned, he pulled up. 'You okay?'

She nodded, at first in reflex, then a second time knowing, remarkably, that she was, indeed, better than fine. Alex was right. She'd always needed to do this at least once, and now, safe in his arms, she knew that she could.

As the water reached higher, she told herself to relax and soon the familiar roll of the waves was lapping her body, as it had so many times before, and Alex was smiling down at her, love and pride shining in his eyes.

'How's that?'

'A little weird,' she admitted, 'but mostly…like I'm saying hello to an old friend.'

His smile said he'd known it all along.

'So how about it, Libby? Will you be my bride?'

Tears slid from the corners of her eyes. Happy tears. Tears that made her feel as if she were the luckiest, most beautiful woman alive.

Alex Wolfe, the man she loved with all her heart, wanted to marry her.

'There's nothing I want more.' She held his bristled jaw in her palm as the gratitude inside her swelled. 'I love you.'

Those gorgeous grey eyes glistened and smiled into hers. 'Say it again.'

As the waves gently lapped, she grazed her thumb over his bottom lip and confessed, 'I love you…like I didn't know existed.'